D0559667

# EARTH
# AND
# *AIR*

# EARTH AND *AIR*

## Tales of Elemental Creatures

by

PETER DICKINSON

**Big Mouth House**
Easthampton, MA

This is a work of fiction. All characters and events portrayed
in this book are either fictitious or used fictitiously.



Big Mouth House
150 Pleasant Street #306
Easthampton, MA 01027
www.bigmouthhouse.net
www.weightlessbooks.com
info@bigmouthhouse.net

Distributed to the trade by Consortium.

First Edition
September 2012

Library of Congress Cataloging-in-Publication Data

Dickinson, Peter, 1927-
Earth and air : tales of elemental creatures / Peter Dickinson. -- 1st ed.
p. cm.
Summary: "Changelings, gryphons, and gods get in the way of us mortals who are struggling to find someone to fall in love with, something interesting to do, somewhere to run to"-- Provided by publisher.
ISBN 978-1-61873-058-9 (hardback) -- ISBN 978-1-61873-038-1 (trade paper) -- ISBN 978-1-61873-058-9 (ebook)
[1. Supernatural--Fiction. 2. Trolls--Fiction. 3. Mythology, Greek--Fiction. 4. Animals, Mythical--Fiction. 5. Goddesses--Fiction.] I. Title.
PZ7.D562Ear 2012
[Fic]--dc23
2012023764

"The Fifth Element" was originally published in slightly different form as "Who Killed the Cat?" in *Verdict of 13* (Julian Symons, ed., Harper & Row, 1979).

Text set in Minion Pro.
Printed on 50# Natures Natural 30% PCR Recycled Paper by C-M Books in Ann Arbor, MI.

# Contents

*For ROBIN*

# Preface

TWENTY-ODD YEARS AGO, NOT LONG after Robin McKinley and I decided that we should get married and she should come to live with me in England, she was asked to write a short story about a mermaid. She didn't have any ideas, so one fine evening we walked down to the village pub to try and think something up over supper. By the time we came home in the twilight we not only had several possible mermaid plots but also a grandiose scheme to collaborate on four collections of short stories about the mythical beings who inhabit the four natural elements: earth, air, fire and water.

I was in the middle of a full-length novel at the time, and when it got stuck, as novels tend to, instead of brooding on the problem I put it aside and wrote a story about a witch's broomstick. I decided it would do for a start, so I put it in a drawer and went back to my novel. Next time I got stuck I did the same thing. The stories began to accumulate.

Robin had more of a problem. Her stories kept turning into full-length novels. The world would be a poorer place without them, but it meant that though we started about 1995, we didn't get our *Water* volume published till 2002. *Fire* took another seven years. I couldn't really complain, as one of my own stories had stretched itself into *The Tears of the Salamander*.

But I am now eighty-four. At this rate I'd be ninety-seven by the time *Earth* sees the light of day. I have no intention of hanging around that long, so when her current novel, *Pegasus,* originally begun as a contribution to *Air,* turned itself into two volumes, then three, I persuaded her to let me see if I could find a home for my long-finished stories about the other two elements.

Here they are.

—PD

PS On the excuse that the alien creatures of science fiction fulfil the same imaginative need as the creatures of myth did for our ancestors, outer space being their element, I have included as a make-weight a story I wrote even before these as a contribution to an anthology with the brief that all the stories must some way or other concern a jury.

# Troll Blood

MARI WAS A SEVENTH CHILD, by some distance—an afterthoughtlessness, her father was fond of remarking. Moreover she had the changeling look, as if she had come from utterly different stock from her parents and siblings, with their traditionally Nordic features, coarsely handsome, with strong bones, blond hair, and winter-blue eyes. Mari was dark-haired, slight, with a fine, almost pearly skin that burnt in the mildest sun. Her face seemed never quite to have lost the crumpled, simian look of the newborn baby. Her mouth was wide, and her eyes, which might more suitably have been brown to go with her colouring, were of an unusual slaty grey.

This look, though only occasionally manifesting itself, ran in the family as persistently as the more normal one. There were likely to be one or two examples in any group photograph in the old albums—a grandmother, a great uncle killed in the Resistance in the Second World War, somebody unidentified in a skiing party way back in the twenties.

There was a story to go with the look. Thirty-odd generations ago a young woman was bathing in a lake when a troll saw her and took her to his underwater cave. Her handmaiden, hiding among the trees, saw what happened and carried the news to the young woman's father. Her mother was dead, and she was his only child. He at once ran to the place and dived into the lake carrying an inflated goatskin weighted down with his armour and weapons. Breathing from the bag through a straw he found the cave, armed himself, and fought the monster until it fled howling. Then he brought his daughter safely home. Nine months later, while her father was away, the young woman bore a son, so clearly marked as a troll that everyone assumed that he would kill the little monster as soon as he returned. But the young woman stole from her room with the child wrapped in her cloak, and met him on the road and begged for his blessing on his grandson, saying, "Your blood is in the boy. If he dies, I will bear no more children." The father took the child from her and unwrapped the cloak and saw for the first time the grandson his daughter had given him. He turned and dipped his finger into a puddle by the road and made the cross of baptism on the baby's forehead. When the child did not scream at the touch of the holy symbol he said, "Whatever his face, there is a Christian soul beneath," and he gave him his blessing.

Even as a child Mari had disliked this story. She of course knew it was only a fairy story, but without being able to formulate the idea she felt in her bones that the problem was not that it was false, but that it was fake. Later, when she had learnt more about such things, she realised that it was probably only a product of the great nineteenth century Nordic folk revival, amalgamating several genuinely old elements—the abduction, the underwater journey, the fight with the cave monster—and tacking on the utterly inappropriate Christianising ending that she had so hated from the first. Be that as it may, that was how the look was said to have come into the family. They called it troll blood.

Mari's parents were second cousins, in a generation of small families among whom the look had had less chance of showing up, so, because they both carried the gene, the whole clan took an unusual interest in the birth of each of their children, only to be disappointed six times in succession. When Mari had at last been born, with the look instantly recognisable, her parents sent round the birth cards saying "To Olav and Britta Gellers, a troll-daughter."

It was a family in which everyone had a nickname. Mari's, from the first, was Troll. She was used to it and never found it strange or considered its meaning, though differences from her brothers and sisters continued to appear. Their style, and that of their parents, was extrovert, cheerfully competitive. They camped, sailed, skied, climbed rocks. The eldest brother just missed representing Norway at long-distance swimming. Two sisters did well in local slalom events. And they were practical people, their father a civil engineer specialising in hydroelectrics, their mother a physiotherapist. The children studied engineering, medicine, accountancy, law. They were not unintelligent, but apart from the acquisition of useful knowledge their academic interests were nonexistent. Their aesthetic tastes were uniformly banal.

All these things were expressive of a more basic difference of character, of life attitude. They threw themselves into things. Mari held herself apart. This was not because she was cold or timid, but because she was, perhaps literally, reserved.

"She is keeping herself for her prince," her mother used to say, only half teasing.

Mari went along with all the family activities, well enough not to be a drag on them, but seldom truly participated. She seemed to have no urge to compete, though she might sometimes do so inadvertently, pushing herself to her physical limits for the mere joy of it. She was an excellent swimmer, with real potential according to her brother's coach, but she saw no point in swimming as fast as she could in a prescribed style in a lane in a big pool with other girls doing the same on either side. She thought it a waste of time in the water. In any case she didn't much care for swimming pools. She liked the sea or a lake or river, in which she could swim in the living current or among the slithering waves, as a seal does, or a gull.

Her academic career, though just as alien to the family ethos, was less of a surprise. She'd always been, by their active, engaged standards, a dreamy child, so they were prepared for her bent to be chiefly literary and were only mildly puzzled that as she moved up through her schools and was more able to choose her courses of study her interests moved steadily back in time, until at University she took Old Norse as a special subject, concentrating on the fragmentary and garbled remains of the earliest writings in the language.

Doctor Tharlsen taught this course, a classically dryasdust bachelor scholar who conscientiously performed his teaching duties, but by rote, while all his intellectual energies were reserved for his life's work, on which he had been engaged for the last twenty years, the reconstruction of MS Frählig 1884. This is what remains of a twelfth century copy of a miscellaneous collection of older MSS in Old Norse. It has some unusual features, the most striking of which is explained (as far as can be made out, since the whole volume is badly damaged by fire) in a Latin introduction by the copyist himself. The MSS he copied must already have been in the library of the Great Cistercian abbey of Dunsdorf, and the then Prince-Abbot, Al[fgardt?] had expressed a wish to know what they were about. The opportunity seems to have arisen with the arrival of a novice from Norway, who was promptly trained as a copyist and set to the task of translation. Thus the MS is interleaved with his attempts to fulfil his brief, with the ancient text on one page and the Latin facing it. The word *attempts* is relevant. Not only was much of the original texts characteristically obscure, but the copyist's grasp of Old Norse was uncertain, and he knew no more Latin than he needed to read a missal. The Prince-Abbot can have been little the wiser after seeing the result. Nevertheless the manuscript was handsomely bound up, and remained in the library until drunken Moravian soldiery looted and fired the abbey after the battle of Stadenbach in 1646. It then disappeared for three hundred years, only coming to light when American troops were billeted at Schloss Frählig at the end of the Second World War, and one of the officers who in civilian life had been a dealer in mediaeval manuscripts recognised the arms of the Prince-Abbot on the spine of the charred volume. How it had come to Frählig remains a mystery.

Externally the damage does not look too serious, but this is not the case. The volume's relationship to the fire was such that, from the first few leaves on, the outer edge of every page was rendered illegible, while the section nearer the spine can still be read, though often with difficulty. The damaged portion increases steadily throughout the volume, so that by the end all but the last few letters of each line on the verso sheet, and the first few on the recto, is lost.

It can be seen that since the material is repeated in translation, page by page, each spread notionally still contains lines whose first part can be read in the original language and second part in Latin, or vice versa, and that from these materials it might in theory be possible to make at least a tentative reconstruction of what the whole original might have been. In 1975 funds were made available for Doctor Tharlsen to undertake the task. He had done little else since then.

Doctor Tharlsen didn't include the Frählig MS in his course, as being far too obscure and difficult, even in the sections for which he had so far published a reconstructed text. If a student happened to mention it he tended to assume that this was an attempt to curry favour, or to show off. This was his first thought when he started to read the separate note Mari had attached to an essay she had handed in. It concerned a paper he had published several years earlier, with the suggested text for a collection of riddling verses from the earlier part of the MS. Mari pointed out that an alternative reading of the Latin would result in a rather more satisfactory riddle. Doctor Tharlsen had already considered the possibility, rejecting it on grounds to do with the technicalities of versification. Still, her suggestion struck him as highly intelligent, and since the rest of her work showed a distinct *feel* for the difficult subject, he for once suggested that a student should remain after class to talk about it. Or rather, two students. With characteristic caution he asked one of the other young women to stay as well, lest there should be any misunderstandings.

The friendship that followed was not as unlikely on his part as it may seem. There were perhaps half a dozen people in the world, none of them among his colleagues at the university, capable of talking to Doctor Tharlsen on equal terms about the Frählig MS. As for the students, he felt with some justice that he would be wasting both his time and theirs if he had bothered them with it. It took him a while to be persuaded that this was not also the case with Mari, but once he realised that her interest was more than passing, his life changed. His energies for the task, jaded by long isolation, returned. Fresh insights came to him, sometimes spontaneously, sometimes in the course of explaining some current problem to her, and more than once stimulated by a suggestion of hers. No doubt this rejuvenation owed something to the fact that she was an attractive young woman, but he continued, despite her protestations, to insist that his housekeeper was always at least in earshot when she came to his rooms.

Mari's side of the relationship is harder to account for, since the true attraction for her was not to Doctor Tharlsen, though she both liked and admired him, but to the Frählig MS itself. Finding in a textbook a footnote reference to one of the riddles, she had felt an intense and instant impulse to know more. The more she learnt, the stronger her feeling became that the book somehow *spoke* to her. She never saw the object itself. That was in a library attached to Yale University. Doctor Tharlsen had studied it there several times over the years, but at home had to work from facsimiles. Confronted even with these ghosts of the real thing Mari felt an excited reverence, while at the same time being appalled by the difficulties it presented.

From the first it was obvious to her that these would be enormously eased by the use of a computer. Doctor Tharlsen knew this in his heart, but had persuaded himself that he was too old to learn to use one. He had a tiresome liver complaint. He doubted that he had many more years to live, and felt he couldn't spare the time to become proficient enough to make real use of the promised advantages, and even then there would be the enormous labour of putting onto the system the mass of material he had so far accumulated. Two years at least, he told himself. No, he must plod on.

"I'll do it for you," Mari told him. "Of course I'll get some things wrong, but I don't think it'll be too bad."

"No, I can't accept that. It would interfere too much with the rest of your work."

"This is more important."

"No, I really can't accept it, Miss Gellers."

"Please, Doctor Tharlsen."

(Doctor Tharlsen maintained a formal relationship with his students, and Mari had guessed early on that he would be embarrassed by anything that suggested his friendship with her was other than straightforwardly professional.)

As a compromise he agreed that she might stay on at the university through the summer vacation and make a start on the work to see how it went. He spent the first three weeks at Yale, where the library had recently installed a new fluoroscopic technique, combined with computerised image enhancement, to extract meaningful characters from damaged documents, and were eager to try it out on the Frählig MS. By the time he returned Mari had the legible parts of the *Gelfunsaga* on disc, including a whole series of extensions of lines revealed by the fluoroscope—on Mari's suggestion he had asked an assistant at the library to email these to her. By the end of the vacation Doctor Tharlsen was himself online and exchanging email with distant colleagues.

A word about the *Gelfunsaga*. This is the longest, most exciting, and at the same time most tantalising portion of the whole MS. Like Snorri's later *Prose Edda*, it appears to be a prose recension of a much older verse legend, from which it occasionally quotes a few lines. The story it seems to tell is referred to nowhere else in the literature. It would clearly be of interest to the general reader, as well as to scholars. Unfortunately it is the last item in the MS, and so the most extensively damaged, less than half of any line being legible. And its being largely in prose inhibits reconstruction, for two reasons: the alliterative verse line of, for instance, the riddles obeys rules almost as strict as the rhymed and scanned lines of later European poetry, and these usefully limit the possibilities for supplying missing words and phrases; and then the copyist, though he had written the Norse verse sections out to fill every line and had translated them into prose, had marked the line endings on both sheets with a slash, thus relating them clearly to each other. Sometimes one half of the meaning could be read in each language. There was no such guide for the prose of the *Gelfunsaga*, and the copyist cannot have recognised the brief verse sections as such, and so failed to mark them.

The story, as far as it can be made out, has affinities with the first two episodes of *Beowulf*. The hero, Gelfun, to rid the neighbourhood from the depredations of a monster (who may or may not be the troll twice referred to in the surviving portions of the text—the Latin uses the word *monstrum* throughout, but at one point adds the epithet *sol timens*, presumably the copyist's attempt at *sunfearer*), goes to the underwater lair of the beast, using a hollow reed(?) to breathe through. His weapons are useless to him, since the creature's limbs are made of rock. (This is one of the passages where the Latin and Norse complement each other enough to make the gist fairly clear.) Gelfun then wrestles with it, apparently inconclusively (the text is once more very obscure), and there is then an exchange of oaths. But he seems to have won the contest, because he takes a treasure of amber from the cave, and then puts the monster onto a ship and dispatches it to sea. The final section is the most seriously damaged part of the manuscript. It seems to have little relation to what went earlier, but apparently deals with Gelfun's choice of an heir.

Because of its near intractability Doctor Tharlsen had kept the *Gelfunsaga* till last. At the time Mari came into his life he was about to start serious work on it.

All this occurred in the summer of Mari's second year at University. For the last fortnight of that long vacation she joined her family at their holiday home on one of the northern fjords. There, disruptingly, she fell in love.

*Fell,* for once, is the right word. The event was as unforeseen and overwhelming as the collapse of a cliff face, altering the whole landscape of her life. She had, of course, had a few tentative involvements with fellow students during the last two years, trial runs, as much to explore her own emotional responses as the physical sensations, and had found, even when the sensations had been enjoyable enough, that the event had left her dissatisfied. She was, she came to realise, one of those people who need to commit themselves, heart and soul as well as body, to anything of importance they undertake. Before she could love, she must choose, choose with her whole being, for all of her life.

She had expected, or at least hoped, to do so as she did most things, deliberately, to find a man of her own age whom she liked, get to know and admire him, while he did the same with her, and then, as it were, build their lifelong love together step by step, much as she had watched her parents and elder siblings building the house on the fjord together. The last thing she had looked for was a cliff-fall.

Dick Vesey was an Englishman, like her father a hydroelectric engineer. They had met at a conference and liked each other, and since Dick's main interest outside his work was fishing, Mari's father had invited him to the fjord for the late salmon run. He was twelve years older than Mari, with her sort of build, slight and active, but his face was different, the skull squarish, and the features moulded in definite angular planes. (One night on their honeymoon, tracing those planes with her fingertips, she wondered aloud whether his parents had conceived him in a bed with a Braque painting on the wall above it. "Far from it," he answered. "It was on open moorland during a cycling trip in the Cheviots, I believe. They didn't intend it to happen. She was married to another man, and didn't want to divorce him.") The effect was to give him a misleadingly merry look, almost droll. In fact he laughed seldom and spoke little. His humour when he chose to deploy it was dry and understated, but quirky, poised between the gnomic and the surreal. Occasionally he produced a remark that might have come straight out of the riddles. He was an excellent and attentive listener. When Mari told him about her work with Doctor Tharlsen, though he had no knowledge of the languages involved, he not only grasped the difficulties but, as her family never in their heart of hearts had done, accepted the importance of the work. She used her laptop to show him some examples of what she was doing. It was while they were sitting together gazing at a laptop screen filled with fragmentary lines of runes that Mari realised what had happened to her.

Later she came to feel that the occasion had not been random, as it had seemed at the time, but utterly appropriate, almost willed. She had fallen for Dick because something about him spoke to her, just as the Frählig MS had, but even more urgently and insistently. The same, he said later, had happened to him, but since each felt there wasn't the slightest chance of the other returning feelings so irrational, they had managed to conceal it from each other.

But not, it turned out, from anyone else. As they waved his car away and watched it vanish behind the pines Mari's father said to her, "Well, when does he propose?" and the rest of the family—ten, including a brother and sister-in-law—bellowed with cheerful northern laughter.

They became engaged by email. She visited him in Scotland over the New Year, staying in a hotel near Dumfries because he had no home of his own but lodged wherever his current work happened to be. Nor was there any family for her to meet. His mother had returned to her husband soon after he was born, the husband making it a condition that she didn't bring the baby, so his father had brought him up, marrying when he was five, but had had no more children, and had then emigrated to Canada with Dick's stepmother when Dick was a student. Dick was now between jobs, and the reason he had chosen Dumfries was that it would allow them to look for a house within easy reach of his next one, which involved the installation of a small hydroelectric plant in the hills above the town. They narrowed the field down drastically by telling the agents that the property must have fishing rights attached. They found nothing they liked.

The failure didn't seem to matter. They spent their eight days together in a state too deep and broad and solid-seeming to be called excitement, too electric with the passing seconds to be called just happiness or contentment. Kissing Dick good-bye at the barrier, turning away, walking through the passport check, Mari felt as if she were putting herself into a coma until she next saw him, able to move, talk, eat, think, but no longer to feel as she had felt while with him, technically alive only.

Superstitiously, Mari hadn't told Doctor Tharlsen of her engagement before her visit to Scotland. Though emotionally certain what she wanted, the sheer irrational force of it seemed to put her into a realm where there are powers that must not be taken for granted, or they will suddenly withhold what they had seemed to give. She and Doctor Tharlsen had assumed that she would be staying on after completing her degree, to work for a Ph.D. on some aspect of the Frählig MS, and thus continue to help him. Why bother him with the unsettling news before it became a certainty in the rational, bread-and-butter world?

Outwardly he took it well, congratulated her, grasped her hands and kissed her gently on the forehead. Without thought she released her hands and hugged him, as she and her family had hugged each other when she had told them the same news. After a few seconds he eased himself from her grasp and sat down. His mouth worked painfully for a moment or two, but he controlled it.

"I am happy for you," he managed to say. "Very happy. All this"—he shrugged towards his littered desk—"is nothing beside it."

Mari dropped to her knees and took his hands again.

"Oh no!" said Mari. "No, please! If I thought marrying Dick meant I couldn't go on helping you, I . . . I don't know what I'd have done."

This, she realised with a shock, was literally true. Her love for Dick filled and suffused her world. It was the light she saw by, the smell of the air she breathed. But so, more gently, odourless as oxygen, a waveband beyond the visible spectrum, did the Frählig MS. Without either one of them, she would become someone else. Someone less. Moreover, though there was no logical or causal connection between them, through her, inexplicably but certainly, they were interconnected.

"You've got to finish it," she said. "You're nearly there. It's just the *Gelfunsaga* now."

He drew a large yellow handkerchief from his breast pocket, wiped his eyes, blew his nose, and smiled at her.

"Yes," he said in his usual voice. "We will finish it. Between us. And you will take your children into your lap and read them our *Gelfunsaga.*"

Dick found their house. It had been a ghillie's cottage, but had fallen into ruin. New owners of the estate had started to do it up for holiday lets, but had overstretched themselves and their bank had called in its loans. It wasn't actually on the market, but Dick had spotted it, fishing, asked about it, and found that the receivers of the estate, to get a minor problem off their hands, would let him have a three-year lease provided he completed the repairs and refurbishment. Mari dropped everything to fly over and see it, and having done so couldn't then imagine wanting to live anywhere else.

She brought photographs to show Doctor Tharlsen. Though they continued to address each other as formally as before, something had happened between them since she'd told him she was marrying Dick, an unspoken acknowledgement that they were now more than colleagues in the Frählig enterprise. They were friends. Mari guessed it was a relationship unfamiliar to him, and she was careful not to strain it, but he seemed positively to like to hear something of her life and interests outside their work, and they'd fallen into the habit of chatting for a few minutes before they began.

"That's what you see when you come out of the door," she said. "The river's fuller than usual, Dick says, because of the snow melt, though it's nothing like we get here, but there's always plenty of water in it. They've had terrible fishing seasons in a lot of the Scottish rivers for the last few years—hardly any water at all , but this one's fed by several tarns up in the hills—they're using some of them for the plant Dick's building. The fishing isn't all that good, actually, not enough pools and spawning grounds, which is why he could afford a day on it in the first place. And he's not going to get a lot more days like that, poor thing, till we've finished doing up the house. The receivers are being very tough about that, and it'll take every penny we've got."

He looked with appropriate interest at the rest of the photographs, and then they settled to work. But after their next session, as she was leaving, he handed her an envelope. There were three words on it in Old Norse, in his meticulous script. "A season's fishing."

The envelope was unsealed, so she opened it. The cheque inside was made out to Richard Vesey for thirty thousand krone.

He interrupted her protests.

"I beg you, Miss Gellers. I have made enquiries as to the cost. It would give me the greatest pleasure. I have little use for my money, and I needed a suitable present for your husband, that he can enjoy immediately, since you will have to wait for yours. It will give me an incentive to finish."

She telephoned Dick, who, of course, was appalled.

"I'm afraid you're going to have to take it," Mari told him. "My present's going to be his *Gelfunsaga.* That matters to me almost as much as it does to him. He doesn't think he's got that long—his liver's getting worse—and if you don't accept this it'll be a way of telling him we don't think he's going to get it finished. Taking it is an act of faith, if you see what I mean. And listen, the very first thing you can do by way of saying thank you to him is get that telephone line in, so we can be on line from the moment we get back."

"Doubt if we'll get broadband this far out."

"Doesn't matter."

They returned from Iceland to, in Mari's case, thrilling news. While they had been away Doctor Tharlsen had been in Yale, where a new and improved image-enhancer had revealed great stretches of hitherto indecipherable text. He had emailed Mari some of the results. Baffling half-phrases had leaped into sense. Fresh overlaps between the Latin and Norse had made obvious what must have lain in the remaining lacunae. Doctor Tharlsen of course would not bring himself to suggest that the end of his task might now be in sight, but between the lines of his dry text Mari could read his excitement.

Dick had less welcome news. Some results of the seismographic survey had come in, showing an apparent rock fault running across a stretch of the hillside upstream from their house. There was a tarn there that he had planned to incorporate into the hydroelectric scheme. They walked up a winding hill track that evening to look at it. When they reached it Mari caught her breath and stood, staring.

In front of her lay a strange feature like a miniature volcanic crater half way up the hillside, holding in its hollow a still, dark tarn that brimmed almost at her feet. The tarn was fed by several streams from the sunlit hills beyond, and spilt out down to the valley by way of a waterfall. Mari could both see and feel that this was a magical place. Dick, in his very different way, had seemed to sense so too.

"There's something pretty big in here," he'd said. "I'd like to have a go at it some day."

"How can you tell?"

"Just a hunch. You get them. They seem to work."

"What will your scheme do to this? I hope it doesn't spoil it. It's perfect now."

"We've got some very stringent guidelines from the conservation people. We're running everything underground as far as possible, but there's bound to be a bit of upheaval while we're working on it, especially if we have to find a way of filling the fault in. I'm going to have to go into that in detail."

"Well, don't spoil this. It's part of the place."

When they had been back a fortnight Doctor Tharlsen returned to Norway. Mari found a brief email from him waiting for her next morning. For the first time in their correspondence he had permitted himself an exclamation mark. More than one.

"Amazing! The whole of the oath exchange is in Old Story Measure! Terribly garbled, but unmistakable. I realised while on the aeroplane, and worked on it for the rest of the journey. I have the first seventeen lines as certain as they will ever be. I can barely stop to sleep. By Sunday night I may have enough to send you to read at your breakfast on Monday. Perhaps even earlier. Bless you! Bless you! Bless you!"

At first light next day, Dick slithered out from under the sheet, bent over the bed, and kissed Mari's ear.

"Catch me some breakfast," she murmured.

"Don't count on it," he said, kissed her again and left to catch the dawn rise. She lay listening to the hiss of the shower, and relishing her own contentment. She could feel it filling the whole valley, brimming along the hilltops, just as the still summer heat seemed to do. Normally she might have lain like that for the hour or more until sunrise before getting up, but today was clearly going to be a scorcher, literally so in her case by the time the sun had any strength in it, so she allowed herself only as long as it took Dick to finish his shower, and then rose and followed him.

She showered, washing her hair, and dried, then walked naked to the kitchen to make herself some morning tea. She was used to wandering round the house like that. The weather was more than warm enough for it. Even at the weekends there was no likelihood of anyone coming by. The nearest house was two and a half miles down the pot-holed track, with the public road another two beyond that, the entrance clearly marked as private. She brought her cup back to her desk in the living room and switched on her PC to check her email.

While she waited for the server to connect she watched Dick out of the window. Doctor Tharlsen's gift covered a bit over half a mile of the near bank, as far as midstream. The bank plunged steeply down at this point, and continued the slope below the waterline, where the main current had carved out a deep channel, through which it ran steadily, with barely a ripple. No salmon would rise in such water. But a rock shelf jutted out from the further shore, creating broken and turbulent shallows, with stiller pools. Part of this reached within Dick's rights, and the river baillie had told him that good fish had been caught here, and had lent him the dinghy to fish from. Using a rock for an anchor, he could moor in the current, which would then drag the anchor very slowly downstream, so that he could start at the top of the rock shelf and cover the whole length of it and then paddle upstream and begin again. He was now just about to start the process. Mari liked to watch him doing it, because of the characteristically deft fashion in which he accomplished everything on the unsteady little dinghy.

Now he was out in the middle of the river, shipping his oars, letting the current swing the dinghy down towards the shelf, picking up the anchor rock, balancing himself to slip it over the side . . .

Because she was watching, Mari saw exactly what happened. From the very first she was in no doubt about it.

Just he had the rock poised to let go, something reached up out of the water—a four-fingered hand, twice human size, the colour of granite, webbed to the top knuckles—and grasped the gunwale and dragged it violently down into the water. Unprepared, unbalanced by the rock, Dick toppled over. When the splash and pother had cleared he was gone. The empty dinghy bobbled at the end of its rope. His rod was being swept away downstream.

She ran for the door and headlong down the bank, and dived. No thought had taken place, but something in her had guessed at the speed of the current, so that she hit the water about twenty yards below the dinghy. The same something controlled her swimming, prolonging her dive and then driving into a breaststroke as it slowed, so that she could stay submerged as long as her breath held. Her eyes were wide open, searching. Immediately around her the water, a sky-reflecting mirror from above, seemed almost as clear as the outer air, but shaded into dimness at any distance. Straight ahead of her, close in against the rock shelf, on the border between the light and the shadows, something went surging past.

It was almost the same colour as the rock, so she saw it only dimly, and couldn't make out its shape. But its movement, the powerful pulse of the legs that drove it upstream, told her what sort of thing it was. Something like a frog or toad. A toad the size of a large cow. As she fought to follow, the current carried her out of sight.

She surfaced, changed to a racing crawl, and reached the shelf. As soon as the current ran less strongly she turned upstream. As a child, before she'd given up competitive swimming, she'd done better at the longer distances than the sprints. Now, automatically, she struck the fastest pace that came naturally to her. Every few strokes, instead of twisting her head to gasp for air, she kept it submerged, peering for some sign of the thing that had taken Dick.

That was what had happened, she was sure. Again it was the glimpsed movement of the creature that had told her, the action of the near forelimb as it swam—something awkward about it—the other limb wasn't being used to swim with, because it was clutching Dick—clutching effortfully—Dick had been struggling still . . .

There! Less than a glimpse this time, a shadow-shift only, uncertain, but she put on a spurt, not bothering to peer below until she had counted thirty strokes, and then only briefly. But yes, she was gaining. Her heart slammed, the air she gulped rasped in her throat and wasn't enough. By now, if she'd been merely racing, her stroke would have been losing its rhythm, but strength came from somewhere, came with a passionate energy that told her it would keep on coming until she caught up.

She had no thought about what would happen then, no fear for herself. Indeed, since the first violent shock of horror as the grey arm had come out of the water, she'd felt nothing at all except the urgency to do what she was doing, to follow the thing that had taken Dick, and take him back. Nothing else existed, not pain, not exhaustion, not the cold of the deep tarn water, nothing.

Ahead, the nature of the river changed. A steep stream fed in from the left just where the main river spilt down a slope of rock, a natural weir right across its width. Their confluence had scooped out a deep, turbulent pool. Only two days ago Mari had sat beside it under a parasol, reading and thinking and dreaming and watching Dick fish. Now, as she reached its lower edge, the creature that had taken him rose from the water on the further side of the pool, close against a vertical slab of rock that divided the river from the stream. If Mari hadn't seen it emerge she wouldn't have known it was there, or rather, all she'd have seen was a rounded boulder projecting from the water. There was no sign of Dick.

She switched to a breaststroke so that she could watch the creature while she swam towards it. After a couple of strokes either the boulder changed, or her perception of it. An inch above the water two wide-set eyes gazed steadily at her. She swam straight on. It erupted through the surface, turning as it did so, reached up with a long-boned arm, grasped the top of the slab behind it, and heaved itself out of the water, scrabbling for toeholds with paddle feet. Dick's body dangled inert from under its other arm. Without looking back at her it disappeared.

She turned, chose a landing spot, and scrambled out and up the bank. The thing was clearly visible thirty yards up the steep side-stream, its huge-haunched hind limbs driving it on through the tumbling water with a powerful, toad-like waddle. Dick's inert body was draped over its shoulder. Mari's legs were rubbery and stupid with their own sudden weight, but she forced them forward, climbing like the creature straight up the stream bed, rather than try to wrestle her way through the heather thickets on either side.

Mostly the creature was hidden by the cragginess of the slope, but then she'd see it again, though she didn't dare snatch more than the odd glimpse for fear of missing her footing. At first she seemed to be gaining, but then she started to fall back as her muscles drained their reserves away, however her heart slammed and her lungs convulsed in the effort to feed them.

The creature reached a waterfall, paused, and for the first time glanced back, looking, she thought, not at her but at the hilltop behind her. The movement twisted Dick towards her. Just below his head there was a yellowish streak down the dark grey rib cage. The creature turned back and plunged into the white curtain. Through the foam she saw it starting to climb. She couldn't go that way, but there was a heather-free slope to her right which reached to the ledge from which the fall spilt. As she stumbled slantwise across it the creature emerged at the top of the fall, stood erect, and looked back, again not apparently at her, but at the eastern ridge behind her. She saw it clearly against the skyline, lit by the almost risen sun. The yellow streak was gone. With a surge of hope she realised what it had been. Dick's vomit. The jolting of the climb had worked like emergency resuscitation and made him throw up. So he was alive. Oh God, let him not now have choked on it! The thing paused only an instant and hurried out of sight.

Mari knew where it had gone, knowing what lay beyond the ridge. She raced on up, reached the top, and stood there, recovering her breath. Desperate though the haste was, she must wait and do that. Breath might be life, both hers and Dick's.

Now, as she waited, searching the unruffled surface for some clue to where the creature had taken him, the sun rimmed the sky behind her. Its long light sluiced across the tarn. She felt its touch on her shoulders, and knew there was another blazing day coming. An instant connection formed in her mind, without any process of thought. All her life, since she was a small child, she had liked to be up very early on days like this, because later on, as soon as there was any strength in the sunlight, she would need to be indoors, or cowering under a parasol or smearing herself every twenty minutes with sunblock. It was part of her inheritance, her troll blood. And the creature too. In its haste to climb the hillside it hadn't been running from her, but from the sunrise. When it had looked behind it, it hadn't been interested in her pursuit, nor in the hill behind her, but in the light itself, spilling above the far ridge. How much longer before the deadly moment? Sunfearer. Troll.

Though the thing she had seen was nothing like any troll she had read of or imagined, the identification came to her with complete assurance. Furthermore there would be a lair in the tarn, a cave with an underwater entrance. Something like that was necessary anyway, if Dick was to be still alive when she found him. He wouldn't survive more than another few minutes underwater. Where? Not where she stood, on what seemed almost a natural earth dam holding the tarn in against the hillside; but over to her right and beyond, where the higher ground reached the water, was a line of low cliffs.

She stared towards them. There! Close in below the dark rocks, more to her right than straight across, the utterly still surface was broken by a sudden ripple and swirl, much like a large fish might make, rising almost to the surface to take a fly and then changing its mind and twisting suddenly back. There was a dip in the cliff just this side of the place. Using that as a landmark she jogged round the edge of the tarn, deliberately choosing a pace that wouldn't instantly run her out of breath again. She dived in where the cliffs began and swam on, still well below a racing speed. The water was degrees colder than that of the river below. At the point she had marked, she stopped, gulped air, kicked herself upwards, and jackknifed into a dive. In the increasing dimness the cliff ran on down, still almost sheer. A good twenty feet below the surface she reached a floor of black, peaty ooze. She turned to her left, and just before her breath gave out glimpsed ahead of her a darker patch on the vertical rock. Madness to try it now.

She pumped herself to the surface and trod water, gasping for air. As soon as she dared she dived again. Yes, an opening in the rock, a triangular cranny like the entrance to a tent. Counting the seconds she swam straight into the darkness, and on through the blind black water. The tunnel seemed to run almost straight, and she could feel her way by the touch of her fingers against the rock on either side. Sometimes when all the family had been swimming together, they used to have timed contests to see who could stay under water longest. In those days she could last a minute and a half, but not swimming vigorously as she was now. Call it a minute, she thought, or a bit over. It would be quicker coming out. Forty seconds in, then . . . She reached the moment, and swam on.

At fifty-five, well past the point where there was any hope in turning back, she saw a change in the darkness ahead. At sixty the change was faint light. At sixty-eight she broke the surface. Retching for air she stared around.

The light was daylight of a sort, seeping in through a narrow crack overhead. It wasn't a light to see by, no better than might have been shed at night in the open by a half moon behind a layer of cloud. She guessed she must be in some kind of cavern, part of the fault that Dick had talked about, perhaps, but in the dimness she could make out neither walls nor roof. She swam forward a few strokes and her feet touched bottom, a shelving rock ledge. As she climbed from the water the only sounds in the stillness were the heaving of her own breath and the patter of drops falling from her hair and limbs, and their fainter echoes.

Not six feet in front of her, a voice spoke. Not a human voice, a soft, deep, booming sound, a drum note that boomed back at her from the cave walls. But its note of questioning surprise told her that it was articulate speech. The thing in the darkness repeated the sound with a different intonation, this time confirming what it had seen. A single word. The strangeness of the voice blurred the two syllables, but she could hear they had not been English. An echo in her mind repeated the sound, and she knew what the thing had said.

"*Woman?*" And then, "*Yes, a woman.*"

"*Who's there?*" she whispered.

"*I do not tell my name,*" said the voice.

"*Troll,*" she said.

"*Rock-child,*" said the voice, correcting her without anger.

Given its voice to focus on she could make the creature out now, a vague dark mass about six feet from her. Its head seemed to be about level with her own, or a little higher, so she guessed it might be squatting, toad-like, on its haunches just above the waterline. It still hadn't crossed her mind to be afraid, but now a shudder of cold shook her body, and she realised how far she had chilled through, and how little reserve of strength she had left to reheat herself.

"*Where is my husband?*" she said. "*You took him. Give him to me.*"

"*He is here.*"

The creature moved, a sudden sideways shuffle, revealing a paler shape that had lain behind it. Mari waded forward, stumbled up the slope and knelt, feeling for Dick with numbed hands. He was lying facedown on the rock so she heaved him over, felt for his face, and laid her ear against his mouth. Nothing. Her fingers were too frozen to find his pulse, but he too seemed to be deathly cold. She straddled his body and started to pump at his chest.

"*What do you do, woman?*" said the troll.

"*I bring his breath back,*" she panted. "*Else he dies.*"

"*He sleeps,*" said the troll, uninterested.

"*Rock-child,*" she said, gasping the words out between pumps, "*. . . we are . . . sun things . . . Sun's heat . . . gives us life . . . Cold long . . . we die . . .*"

She stopped pumping, knelt by Dick's head, pinched his nose, and forced her breath between his lips. She backed off, let the lungs collapse, and tried again. And again. The effort was warming her, but she had little more to give. Even with her full strength, she wouldn't have been able to keep this up for more than a minute or two. She straddled Dick's body again and resumed pumping.

"*Go to the sun, then,*" said the troll.

"*I must take . . . my husband . . . under the water . . . Too far . . . we die . . . Oh, troll . . . rock-child . . . help me . . . I am of . . . your blood.*"

Desperate, she flung herself round to breathe again into Dick's mouth. Nothing. Nothing.

A huge, cold hand gripped her shoulder and hauled her upright. It turned her and she found herself facing the creature, held by both shoulders, looking up at the enormous head. The light seemed stronger now. Perhaps the sun had risen far enough to shine further into the opening, but she could make out the wide-set bulbous eyes and the V-shaped mouth that seemed to split the face from side to side.

"*My blood, sun-child?*" boomed the troll.

"*It's a story in my family,*" she gabbled, desperate to get back to Dick, but at the same time not to waste this first apparent wakening of the creature's interest. "*One of my forefathers—his daughter was taken by a troll . . .*" She raced through the first half of the tale . . .

No, not the stupid Christian end—that wouldn't mean anything to it. On impulse, she switched to the fragments that could be gleaned from the *Gelfunsaga*—the inconclusive contest in the cave, the oath-taking—and wrenched herself away, but then crumpled to the floor. She managed to crawl back to Dick but couldn't raise herself to start the resuscitation again. She collapsed against him and lay there.

A voice was booming overhead. With a huge effort she concentrated on the syllables.

"*Child of my blood, rock-born and sun-born, I give you your man back. Go now to your place. Wait there. The sun must set. I will bring him.*"

She managed to raise her head.

"*Rock-child,*" she sighed. "*I am too weary. I cannot swim so far. I cannot hold in my breath so long beneath the water.*"

She felt herself being turned over and lifted. With limp muscles she struggled against the creature's grip.

"*My man will die,*" she protested. "*It is too cold in this place.*"

"*Woman, we are oath-bound,*" said the creature. "*He will live. I will bring him this dusk. Now, breathe deep.*"

She closed her eyes as it carried her into the water, and concentrated on making her breath last as long as possible. As soon as they were under the surface it shifted her to beneath its left arm so that her body could trail against its own. She could feel the steady driving pulse of its hind limbs, and tell from the flow of the water against her skin that they were moving faster than any human swimmer could have done. It wasn't long before the grip changed again, held her beneath the arms, pushed her forward and let go. As she opened her eyes she was already swimming.

There was light ahead. She was at the tunnel mouth. Weakly she swam on and up to the silvery surface.

She made it to the shore beyond the cliffs and climbed out, shuddering, too weak to stand. But the sun was warm enough now to be some use, and life began to come back to her as she crawled round the edge of the tarn. By the time she reached the outflow she could just about totter to her feet. Painfully she climbed down the way she had come, first across the grassy slope by the waterfall and then in the stream bed. By the time she reached the pool at the bottom she could feel her skin beginning to scorch. She slid into the water, and barely bothering to swim let the current carry her home.

Already she had decided there was nothing she could do except trust the creature and wait till nightfall. No point in going for help, to the police, to the water-baillie. How could she hope to persuade them that though Dick had fallen into the river just outside the house the place to look for him was in the tarn halfway up the hill? But at least she could get herself warm, and then fed, and rested. She went to the bathroom and turned on the shower. As the kindly heat seeped into her she realised there was indeed something she could do.

There was no instant hurry. Doctor Tharlsen had set times for all he did. He wouldn't look at his email until Helge brought in his luncheon tray. Mari went into the kitchen, turned on the kettle, made herself a pot of tea and a Marmite sandwich, and carried them into her desk. Her patient window cleaner was still repetitively saving her screen. "Thanks," she whispered, as always, when the touch of her hand on the mouse made him vanish.

She had post, but not from Doctor Tharlsen. Monday, he'd said. She downloaded, not bothering to read more than the subject headings, wrote out her brief message and sent it off. Then she finished her sandwich, set the alarm, and lay down on the bed, not knowing whether she would sleep or not. She did so, almost instantly, and forgot everything.

It came back the moment the alarm went. She went at once to the PC. While she waited for the server to connect she looked, just as she had done that morning, out of the window. Noon blazed down on the moving river. The dinghy bobbled, empty, on its rope—without Dick's weight in it the current flowed smoothly beneath it and it hadn't shifted more than a few paces downstream. She herself felt like that, empty, weightless, with a powerful current sweeping by and herself unable to do more than float on its surface, waiting, waiting . . .

The server connected. Yes, she had post. Only the line of her address, and the note that there was an attachment. Her fingers moved steadily over the keys, and the text came up. Runes, of course, four four-line verses, one more line of verse and three of prose. She started to read, translating in her head as she went.

*Then spoke Raggir, the rock-born marvel,*
*"No longer yours, O Jarl, is the woman.*
*"Mine I have made her in my mountain hall.*
*"A dark cave her body. There breeds my son."*

*Answered Gelfun, "Goblin, sun-fearer,*
*"From me you take a treasure of amber.*
*"No gold in my hoard is half so precious.*
*"Let her say farewell, have a father's blessing."*

*At his knee the woman knelt for his hand.*
*By the hair he grabbed her, grasped the bright ringlets,*
*Fiercely lifted her, laid her against him.*
*Lean at her neck his knife glinted.*

*Then said Gelfun, grimly mocking,*
*"Does she die here, demon? Dies your son also.*
*"Does she come with me from the mid-earth darkness*
*"To bear your son in the sweet daylight?"*

*Raggir the rock-born roared in his anger . . .*

*This is as much as I am sure of. The actual oaths are still mainly conjectures, too much so for me even to guess at their gist. Let me know if you need them also. It will take a while to transcribe into a form you can make any kind of sense out of. I must go out now. If you are free this evening, call me and tell me what this is about. I am troubled for you.*

E.L.T.

Mari turned away, weeping. She longed to speak to him. He wouldn't doubt her. There was no one else of whom she could say that, not even her own family. She told herself she must get her strength back, so made lunch of a sort and forced it down, but this time couldn't sleep, and after a while got up and dusted and cleaned the bedroom and living room and scrubbed the kitchen floor and polished Dick's shoes and her own high boots, painfully hauling the dreadful minutes by. As she worked she wondered what she was going to tell people if the creature didn't keep its promise. That Dick had gone fishing somewhere out of sight and not come back in the evening? By now she would have started to search, surely. It was only a half mile of river. His waders were still in the house. If he'd fallen in from the bank he'd have left some trace, his net, gaff, creel . . . Her mind wouldn't stick to the problem. The creature kept dragging it back to the cave.

She was unable to eat any supper. It was still too warm an evening for anything but shorts and a loose blouse, so as soon as the sun slid below the ridge opposite she smeared herself with mosquito repellent and went out and sat on the bank and waited. A little downstream the stupid dinghy bobbled at the end of its rope. It crossed her mind to fetch it ashore, but that would mean putting the mosquito cream on again, so she left it. She assumed that the creature would carry Dick back as it had taken him, swimming down the river, and bring him ashore where she sat. The current moved soundlessly past, its surface sometimes heart-stoppingly broken by the rise of a fish. Each time, as the swirl broke the smoothness, she thought it was the creature beginning to surface, and then knew that it wasn't. Hope faded with the fading light. It was almost dark when she heard the click of a dislodged pebble, and turned and saw Dick stumbling towards her down the track from the top of the valley.

She rose and ran up the bank and flung her arms round him.

"Oh, darling," she whispered.

He didn't reply, but hugged her clumsily in return. He seemed utterly dazed, unsure where he was, who she was. He found his way beneath her blouse, and his hands began to explore her back as if for the first time. They were stone cold, and her body refused to respond. She had to will herself not to shrink from his touch, and then to answer his caress. Through the fabric of his shirt she could feel the chill of his body. Stone cold. She slid her fingers up, as always when they started an embrace, to the inner edge of his right shoulder blade, and found the little nodule, like an old scar, where the skin dipped towards the spine. It was a birth defect, apparently, that ran in his family. Some rearrangement of the nerves beneath made it supersensitive to touch, causing him to sigh and half shrug the shoulder as she stroked it. Not now. Too stone cold, even for that.

Stone cold. He shouldn't be alive, or at least in a coma. Stone.

"*Rock-born,*" she whispered. And then, continuing the guess, "*Raggir.*"

His hands stopped moving. She loosed her hold on him, took him by the elbows, and pushed herself away. He didn't resist.

"*Where is my husband?*" she asked softly.

"*He is here also.*"

It was Dick's voice, but not a language Dick knew. She wasn't surprised, or angry, or frightened. Her mind seemed utterly clear. There was still one hope only, and she knew how she must achieve it.

"*No,*" she said again. "*I must have my husband. Him only. Listen, Raggir, rock-born, and I will tell you a tale. Long ago, in a country across the sea, you took a woman to your cave. She was Gelfun's daughter. Gelfun came to your cave. You said, 'This woman is mine now. She carries my son in her womb.' Gelfun took her. He put his knife to her throat. He said, 'Give her back to me or I kill her, Then your son dies also. But let me take her, and I will raise your son as mine.' You and he swore oaths and made it so. Now I, Mari, of the lineage of Gelfun, say this. Take me, rock-born, by guile or by force, put your seed into me, and I will kill myself, as Gelfun would have killed his own daughter. Then you will lose both your new child and your old child, by whom your blood is in me. But give me back my husband, him alone, him living, and I will give you a gift as great to you.*"

He stood for a while, simply looking at her in the late twilight.

"*Do you drive me from my place, as Gelfun drove me?*" he asked. "*He would have brought an army of men, to dig out the rocks, to drain my lake away, to beset my cave and take me and bind me with chains and drag me into the sun. I am the last of my kind. Therefore I took the ship he gave me and came to this land. Long I lived sadly before I found my cave. I would not live so again.*"

"*This is my gift to you,*" said Mari, and explained to him as best she could about the hydroelectric scheme. He didn't seem to find it strange.

"*It is in my husband's hands,*" she finished. "*At his word it will be done or not done. Therefore he must live, so that I may persuade him.*"

"*Unfasten the boat,*" he said. "*Take it to the rock in the middle of the river. Wait there.*"

He turned and walked down the bank. At the river's edge he leaped, frog-fashion, into the water.

Mari stripped off and followed. Reaching the dinghy she used the anchor rope to haul herself down to the river bed, untied the anchor rock by feel, and surfaced gasping. Then she turned on her back and kicked across the current to the stiller water close by the rock shelf. Once there she could take it more easily, simply maintaining her position. The first she knew of the creature's return was the boom of its voice close behind her.

"*That is good. Stay there.*"

Nothing happened for a while, though she could tell from the slackened current that the creature was still there, sheltering her from its flow. She assumed it must be doing something concerned with separating itself from Dick's body, though it was already speaking in its own voice, not his. Then it grunted and she heard the splash of its heaving itself up onto the shelf. It waddled past her with Dick inert in its arms and lowered him into the dinghy.

"*Child of my blood, farewell,*" it boomed. "*I leave you with a choice.*"

It leaped neatly into the water and disappeared.

Mari towed the dinghy ashore, somehow heaved Dick out onto the bank, and dragged him on up and into the house. By the time she had got him into the living room she was almost spent. She knelt beside him and felt for his pulse. It was there, faint and slow. She switched on all the heaters, stripped off his sodden clothes, dried him and rolled him into a duvet, flung another one over him, and then dried herself and wriggled in beside him, holding him close, trying to warm him through with her own warmth. Now she could actually feel the movement of his breathing. She slid her hand under him, felt for the cicatrice and stroked it gently. His shoulder stirred and she heard his sigh.

He slept almost till noon next day, but Mari woke at the usual time, slipped out of bed and stole away to her desk. There was a long email from Doctor Tharlsen, with further fragments from the oath-taking passage of the *Gelfunsaga*. Several of them now slid into place. Likely links emerged. She wrote back briefly:

*Take this for the moment as a dream. It was not, but I would rather not tell you in writing, even in runes. I have met Raggir. He took Dick, and I followed and took him back, using the same threat Gelfun used about killing his daughter. I couldn't have done it without you. This is what Raggir told me about what happened next. It is not the words of the MS, but the gist of the events. You will see where it fits . . .*

When she had finished her account she went to *Britannica Online* and read up about the mating behaviour of the amphibia.

"What happened?" said Dick as he wolfed his way through an enormous breakfast. "Something tipped the dinghy over. That's the last I remember."

She had never lied to him, and wouldn't do so now.

"I'll tell you this evening," she said.

She did so in the dusk, sitting at the edge of the tarn, with the stream beside them racing towards the waterfall.

"I suppose you could get a wetsuit and oxygen mask and go down and find the cave," she said as she finished. "I think I'd have to go first and ask his permission. Otherwise I don't know what he'd do."

"I don't need to," he said. "I would have believed you in any case, but in fact I saw his arm come out of the water, only I thought I was hallucinating. What did he do it for? Trolls eat people, don't they?"

"He needed you alive. He is the last of his kind. He told me that. He can't father any more trolls, but he's found a way of passing something on. Look at me. I'm human all through, but I still have troll blood. Look how I scorch in the sun. That's inherited from him. He wanted to come to me in your body—I don't know how he does that—he made himself into a rock for a moment or two when he came out of the pool at the bottom, but that isn't the same thing. I don't think we're the first ones. I think he looks in through people's windows at night. He wasn't at all surprised when I told him about electricity.

"Anyway, he was going to make love to me in your body and we'd have a baby. It would still have been your child—I don't believe he and I could actually cross-breed, we're too different—but he'd have passed something on again—troll blood on both sides . . ."

"You know, I have a sort of dream memory of walking towards you. It was almost dark. You ran to meet me and we hugged each other, and then you suddenly pushed me away."

"He said you were there too."

"I'm still believing all this. It's an act of faith."

"But you are believing it?"

"I think I have to . . . there's something else?"

"Yes . . . This is . . . well, see what you think. I read up about frogs and toads and so on this morning. Most of them mate in water. The female releases the eggs and the male fertilises them. I told you he made me go and fetch the dinghy and take it to the rock shelf. I waited for a bit, and then he popped up close behind me and just stayed there for two or three minutes before he climbed out and put you in the dinghy . . ."

Her voice had dropped to a shaky whisper with the strain of telling him. He took her hand and looked at her with his characteristic half-tilt of the head.

"Frogs and toads. I've seen them at it. They hug each other pretty close, don't they? And it goes on for hours."

"It was only a couple of minutes. And no, he didn't touch me. But . . ."

"You didn't release any eggs?"

"I'm due to ovulate in a couple of days"

"And then . . .?"

"I think it depends on us. He said he left me with a choice. He can't fertilise me by himself."

"And you want to have the child?"

Mari had managed to suppress consideration of this. What she, personally, wanted had seemed of no importance beside Dick's possible reactions. But now that he himself asked the question, she knew the answer, knew it through every cell in her body. It was as if a particular gene somewhere along the tangled DNA in each cell had at the same instant fired in response.

"I don't know about want . . . oh, darling . . . I just don't know!"

"You feel somehow, as it were, compelled? A moral duty, perhaps?"

His voice was drier, more remote than she had ever heard it.

"Something like that," she whispered.

He thought for a long while, still holding her hand as he stared out across the motionless tarn.

"I meant what I said about faith," he said at last. "If you believe you're right, then I believe too."

"Oh, my darling . . ."

"Do you want me to keep your side of the bargain?"

"If you can find a way."

The birth wasn't abnormal, except that it was far more difficult and painful than even the midwife expected. She sent for a senior colleague to confirm there was nothing more she might be doing, and the colleague stayed to help. Mari was barely conscious when it was over. Her hand was clenched on Dick's and wouldn't let go. Through dark red mists she heard a low-voiced muttering, the younger woman first, doubt and disappointment, and then a reassuring murmur from the older woman. She forced herself to listen and caught the last few words in a strong Scots accent. ". . . a look you get round here. I've seen three or four of them like that, and they've turned out just grand."

They put the still whimpering baby, cleaned and wrapped, into Mari's arms, and she hugged it to her. The mists cleared, and she looked at the wrinkled face, the unusually wide mouth, the bleary, slightly bulging eyes.

"Spit image of you," said Dick cheerfully.

"Troll blood," she whispered.

"Both sides?"

(Gently. Carefully teasing.) She smiled back.

"Just one and a bit," she whispered. "Wait."

She slid her hand in under the wrap and explored for what she had already felt through the thin cloth. Yes, there, on the other shoulder from his, and lower down. Delicately with a fingertip she caressed the minuscule bump in the skin. The whimpering stopped. The taut face relaxed. The shoulder moved in a faint half shrug, and the lips parted in an inaudible sigh of pleasure.

# Ridiki

*For Hazel*

HE FOUND HER BETWEEN THE vine rows on the parched hillside below the farm.

He already knew something must have happened to her. This time of year school started early and finished at midday, and she hadn't been waiting for him in her usual place under the fig beside the gate, at the end of his long his trudge up the hill. Papa Alexi, sitting under the vine by the door of his cottage, hadn't seen her, and everyone else was resting out the heat of the day, so there was nobody about to ask. He'd already spent over an hour looking for her, calling softly so as not to disturb the sleepers, so he was more than half prepared. But not for this.

She was lying on her side. Her lips were drawn back, baring her gums in a mad snarl. Her swollen tongue stuck out sideways at the corner of her mouth. The eye that he could see was as dull as a piece of sea-rubbed glass. Her left foreleg—the one Rania had dropped the skillet on—stuck out in front of her chest as straight as it could ever go, while the other three, and her tail, were all curled up under the tense arch of her body.

When he picked her up everything stayed locked in position, rigid as stubs of branches sticking out from a log. Only as he staggered back up the slope with her—his face a stiff mask, his stomach a stone—the feathery black tip of her tail flicked lightly to the jolt of each step.

"Horned viper," said Papa Alexi, when he showed him. "Got her on the tongue, see? Vicious bite he's got. Much worse than the common one. Kill a strong man. Bad luck, Steff, very bad luck. Nice dog."

He carried her on and laid her down beside the fig tree, covering her body with the old sack she used to sleep on in the corner by the mule shed. He tied the fig branches out of his way, fetched a crowbar and spade, and sweated the rest of the afternoon away prodding and scooping and chopping through roots, picking out the larger rocks from the spoil and setting them aside. When the farm woke and people started to come and go, some of them asked what he was up to. He just grunted and worked on.

By sunset the hole was as deep as the reach of his arm. He changed her everyday collar for her smart red Sunday one with the brass studs, wrapped her in the sack and lowered her into the grave. Gently he covered her with the larger rocks he'd kept, fitting them together according to their shapes and then ramming earth between them in a double layer, proof against any possible scavenger.

Finally he filled in the hole and spread what was left of the spoil back under the fig. The stars were bright by the time he fetched a small flask of oil from the barrel in the larder and poured it slowly over her grave.

"Good-bye, Ridiki," he said. "Good-bye."

He scattered the remaining handful of earth over the grave, let the fig branches back to hide and shelter it, and turned away.

The evening meal was long over, but he couldn't have eaten. He sat until almost midnight on the boulder beside the vegetable patch with her old collar spread between his hands and his thumbs endlessly caressing the wrinkled leather. The constellations wheeled westward and the lights of the fishing-boats moved quietly around Thasos. When he was sure that there'd be no one about to speak to him he coiled the collar tightly in on itself, put it in his shirt pocket, went up to his cot in the loft over the storeroom and lay down, knowing he wouldn't sleep.

But he did, and dreamed. He was following Ridiki along a track at the bottom of an unfamiliar valley, narrow and rocky. She was trotting ahead with the curious prancing gait her bent leg gave her, her whole attitude full of amused interest, ears pricked up and cupped forward, tail waving above her back, as if she expected something new and fascinating to appear round the next corner, some odour she could nose into, some little rustler she could pounce on in a tussock beside the path—pure Ridiki, Ridiki electric with life.

The track turned, climbed steeply. Ridiki danced up it. He scrambled panting after her. The cave seemed to appear out of nowhere. She trotted weightless towards it, while he toiled up, heavier and heavier. At the entrance she paused and looked back at him over her shoulder. He tried to call to her to wait, but no breath would come. She turned away and danced into the dark. When he reached the cave the darkness seemed to begin like a wall at the entrance. He called again and again. Not a whisper of an echo returned. He had to go; he couldn't remember why.

"I'm coming back," he told himself. "I'll make sure I remember the way."

But as he trudged sick-hearted along the valley everything kept shifting and changing. A twisted tree beside the track was no longer there when he looked back to fix its shape in his mind, and the whole landscape beyond where it should have been was utterly unlike any he had seen before.

At first light the two cocks crowed, as always, in raucous competition. He had grown used to sleeping through the racket almost since he'd first come to live on the farm, but this morning he shot fully awake and lay in the dim light of early dawn knowing he'd never see Ridiki again.

He willed himself not to be seen moping. It was a Saturday, and he had his regular tasks to do. Mucking out the mule shed wasn't too bad, but there was a haunting absence at his feet as he sat in the doorway cleaning and oiling the harness.

"Sorry about that dog of yours," said Nikos as he passed. "Nice little beast, spite of that gammy leg, and clever as they come. How old was she, now?"

"Five."

"Bad luck. Atalanta will be whelping any day now. Have a word with your uncle, shall I?"

*I don't want another dog! I want Ridiki!*

He suppressed the scream. It was a kind offer. Nikos was his uncle's shepherd, and his uncle listened to what he said, which he didn't with most people.

"They'll all be spoken for," he said. "He only let me keep Ridiki because Rania had dropped a skillet on her leg."

"Born clumsy," said Nikos. "May be an extra, Steff. Atalanta's pretty gross. Let's see."

"They'll be spoken for too."

This was true. The Deniakis dogs were famous far beyond the parish. Steff's great-grandfather had been in the Free Greek Navy during the war against Hitler, stationed in an English port called Hull, and he'd spent his shore leaves helping on a farm in the hills above the town. There were sheep dogs there who worked to whistled commands, and he'd talked to the shepherd about how they were trained. When the war was over and he'd come to say good-bye the farmer had given him a puppy, which he'd managed to smuggle aboard his ship and home. Once out of the navy he'd successfully trained some of the puppies she'd born to the farm dogs, not to the lip-whistles the Yorkshire shepherds used but to the traditional five-reed pipe of the Greeks.

Now, forty years later, despite the variable shapes and sizes, the colouring had settled down to a yellowish tan with black blotches, and the working instinct stayed strongly in the breed. Steff's uncle could still sell as many pups as his bitches produced, all named after ancient Greeks, real or imaginary. They were very much working dogs, and Nikos used to train them on to sell ready for their work. But for Rania's clumsiness Ridiki would have gone that way, as the rest of the litter had.

All day that one moment of the dream—Ridiki vanishing into the dark, as sudden as a lamp going out—stayed like a shadow at the side of his mind. It didn't change. He had a feeling both of knowing the place and of never having been there before. But if he tried to fix anything outside the single instant, it was like grasping loose sand. The details trickled away before he could look at them.

He fetched his midday meal from the kitchen and ate it in the shade of the fig tree, and then, while the farm settled down to its regular afternoon stillness, went to look for Papa Alexi.

Papa Alexi was Steff's great-uncle, his grandfather's brother. Being a younger son he'd had to leave the farm, and look for a life elsewhere. He wasn't anyone's father, but people called him Papa because he'd trained as a priest, but he'd stopped doing that to fight in the Resistance, and then in the terrible civil wars that had followed. That was when he'd stopped believing what the priests had been teaching him, so he'd spent all his working life as a schoolmaster in Thessaloniki. He'd never married, but his sister, Aunt Nix, had housekept for him after her own husband had died. When he'd retired they'd both come back to live on the farm, in the old cottage where generations of other returning wanderers had come to end their days in the place where they'd been born.

The farm could afford to house them. There were other farms in the valley, as well as twenty or thirty peasant holdings, but Deniakis was much the largest, with Nikos and three other farmhands, and several women, on the payroll, working a large section of the fertile land along the river, orchards and vineyards, and a great stretch of the rough pasture above them running all the way up to the ridge.

Steff found Papa Alexi as usual under the vine, reading and drowsing and waking to read again. Today Aunt Nix was sitting opposite him with her cat on her lap and her lace-making kit beside her.

"You poor boy," she said. "I know how it feels. It's no use anyone saying anything, is it?"

Steff shook his head. He didn't know how to begin. Papa Alexi marked his page with a vine leaf and closed the book.

"But you wanted something from us all the same?" he said.

"Well . . . are there any caves up in the mountains near here? Big ones, I mean. Not like that one on the way to Crow's Castle—you can see right to the back of that without going in."

"Not that I know of," said Papa Alexi.

"What about Tartaros?" said Aunt Nix. "That's a really big, deep cave, Steff. It's on the far side of Sunion."

"Only it isn't a cave, it's an old mine," said Papa Alexi. "Genuinely old. Alexander the Great paid his phalanxes with good Tartaros silver. There were seams of the pure metal to be mined in those days. You know perfectly well you persuaded me to go and look for silver there once."

"Only you got cold feet when it came to crossing into Mentathos land. We were actually looking down at the entrance, Steff . . ."

"You wouldn't have been the one Dad thrashed. Anyway, you knew it was a mine, back then."

"Of course I did. But that doesn't mean it can't have been a perfectly good cave long before it was ever a mine. Nanna Tasoula told me it used to be one of the entrances to the underworld. There was this nymph Zeus had his eye on, only his brother Dis got to her first and made off with her, but before he could get back into the underworld through one of his regular entrances Zeus threw a thunderbolt at him. Only he missed and split the mountain apart and made an opening and Dis escaped down there. That's why it's called Tartaros. Nanna Tasoula was full of interesting stories like that, Steff."

"And you believe in all of them," said Papa Alexi. "You know quite well it was a mine."

They wrangled on, deliberately trying to keep Steff amused, he guessed. He tried to pay attention in a dazed kind of way. All he knew was that he had to go and look at the cave, if only to get rid of the dream. It couldn't be helped that it was on Mentathos land. There'd always been bad blood between Deniakis and Mentathos, and it had been worse since the troubles after the war, when some of the young men had fought on opposite sides, and terrible things had been done. Papa Alexi made the point himself.

"Don't you go trying it, Steff," he said. "It's not only Mentathos being a hard man, which he is, and he'd be pretty rough with you if you were found. He'd make serious trouble with your uncle. His father sold the mineral rights to a mining company. They came, and cleaned out any silver there was to be had. On top of that they've still got the rights, fifty-odd years. No wonder he's touchy about it. Last thing he needs is anyone finding silver again."

"Steff just wants to look," said Aunt Nix. "It's to do with your dream, isn't it, Steff? Tartaros. I bet you that's where it came from, your dream. Eurydice, after all. You remember the story, Steff . . ."

He barely listened.

Of course he knew the story, because of the name, though he hadn't thought about it till now. Ridiki had already been named when he'd got her, so in his mind that's who she was, and nothing to do with the old Greek nymph she was named from. But that didn't stop Aunt Nix telling him again what a great musician Orpheus had been in the days when Apollo and Athene and the other gods still walked the earth; and how he'd invented the lyre, and the wild beasts would come out of the woods to listen enchanted to his playing; and how when his wife Eurydice had died of a snakebite he'd made his way to the gates of the underworld and with his music charmed his way past their terrible guardian, the three-head dog Cerberus, and then coaxed Charon, the surly ferryman who takes dead souls across the river Styx into Tartaros, the underworld itself; and how at last he'd stood before the throne of the god Dis, the iron-hearted lord of the dead, the one living man in all that million-peopled realm, and drawn from his lyre sounds full of sunlight, and the sap of plants and trees, and the pulse of animal hearts, and the airs of summer.

"Then Dis's heart had softened just the weeniest bit," said Aunt Nix, "and he told Orpheus that he'd got to go back where he belonged, but Eurydice could follow him provided he didn't look back to make sure she was there until he stood in the sunlight, or she'd have to go back down to the underworld and he'd never see her again. So back Orpheus went, across the Styx, past the three snarling heads of Cerberus, until he saw the daylight clear ahead of him. But then he couldn't bear it any more, not knowing whether Eurydice was really there behind him, and he looked back over his shoulder to check, and there she was, plain as plain, but he wasn't yet out in the sunlight, and so as he turned to embrace her she gave a despairing cry and faded away into the darkness and he never saw her again."

"I really don't think . . ." said Uncle Alexi.

"Nonsense," said Aunt Nix. "Steff only wants to look. He can do that from above. Like we did, Lexi. You go up the track toward the monastery and turn right at the old sheepfold, and then . . ."

Steff listened with care to her directions.

"Really, this isn't a good idea," said Papa Alexi when she'd finished.

"Please," said Steff. "It's not just I want to. I . . . I've got to."

Papa Alexi looked at him and sighed.

"All right," he said. "Start early. It's a long way, and it'll be hot. Take enough water. There's a stream a little after you turn off at the sheepfold—you can refill your bottle there. You probably won't be back till after dark. Scratch on my shutter when you're home."

He spent the evening writing his Sunday letter to his mother. She lived in Athens, with her new family. He didn't blame her, or even miss her most of the time. She had a little shop selling smart, expensive clothes to rich women. That was what she'd been doing when she'd met his father, who'd worked for the government in the Foreign Ministry. Athens was where she belonged.

Steff didn't remember his father. When he was still a baby some terrorists had tried to set off a bomb under the Foreign Minister's car, but they'd got the wrong car, the one Steff's father had been in, so he didn't remember him at all. He'd no idea what he had thought about things. But he'd been a Deniakis, so Steff was pretty sure he'd felt much the same as he himself did, that he belonged on the farm.

Though he'd spent most of his first five years in Athens, his earliest memory was of sitting on a doorstep holding a squirming puppy he'd been given to cuddle and watching chickens scrattling in the sunlit dust. And then of a shattering, uncharacteristic tantrum he'd thrown on being taken out to the car to go back to Athens. He'd had a stepfather by then, Philip, and a stepsister soon after. Everyone had done their best to make him feel part of this new family, but he hadn't been interested. Time in Athens was just time to be got through somehow. Two or three months there were nothing like as real for him as a few days on the farm, being let help with the animals, harvesting fallen olives, tagging round after his cousins.

By the time he was six his mother was driving him up there at the start of the school holidays, and fetching him when they were over. It had been his idea that he should live there most of the time, going to the little school in the town. She'd come up to see him for a few days at a time, fetch him to Athens for Christmas, take him on the family summer holiday. He got along all right with his steps, and was fond of his mother. She took trouble and was fun to be with. He guessed that she felt much the same as he did, a bit guilty about not minding more.

So he was surprised now to find how much he wanted to tell her about Ridiki. He'd always put something about her in his weekly letters, and she always asked, but this time everything seemed to come pouring out—what had happened, how he'd searched for her, found her, buried her, his misery and despair and utter loneliness. And the dream—Ridiki glancing over her shoulder and vanishing, and him not even being able to say good-bye. He had said good-bye to her once, in the real world, at her graveside. But if he was ever going to let go of her completely he had to do it again in the dream world where she had gone. He mustn't keep anything. He would take her collar, and the shepherd's pipes he'd used to train her, and find somewhere inside the cave to hide them, where they'd never be found, and call his good-byes into the darkness, and go. Then it would be over.

All this he wrote down, hardly pausing to think or rest. He fetched his supper up to his room and wrote steadily on. It was as if his mother was the one person in all the world he needed to tell. Nobody else would do. When he'd finished he hid the letter, unsealed, in his clothes-chest, got everything ready that he'd need for the morning, and went to bed, willing himself to wake when the cocks crew.

Of course he woke several times before that, certain he must have missed their calls, but he didn't when at last they came. He stole down the stairs, put on the clothes that he'd hidden beneath them with his satchel, and left. Hero, the old watchdog, rose growling at his approach, but recognised Steff's voice when he called her name, and lay back down. It was still more dark than light when he set out towards the monastery, making the best speed he could through the dewy dawn air.

He reached the ridge around noon. The last several miles he had sweated up goat paths under a blazing sun. But so far so good. He had started to explore these hillsides as soon as he'd been old enough to follow his cousins around, so he'd found his way without trouble among the fields and vineyards and olive groves on the lower slopes, the rough pastures above them where he, with Nikos's help, had taught Ridiki the business of shepherding, and then, above those, up between the dense patches of scrub that was the only stuff that would grow there.

He stopped to eat and rest in the last of their shade, looking west over the heat-hazed distances of the coastal hills. The main mass of Sunion rose on his right. It wasn't enormous, but it was a true mountain, steep, and for half the year capped with snow that fed the fields and pastures of the valleys below. Even on this southern side the last white streaks had melted from its gullies only a few weeks back. The ridge on which he was sitting climbed towards that peak. Its crest, only fifty paces above him, had been a frontier between the homeland and enemy territory in the long, imaginary history his cousins had constructed for their wars and adventures; and in the real, everyday world that was almost true. The legal ownership of these uncultivatable uplands might be vague, but despite that the ridge was an ancient boundary, well understood by all, between Deniakis and their neighbours and dependants and those of Mentathos. Even in their wildest feats of daring, Paulo, Steff's elder cousin, had never let any of them set foot beyond it. Now he had no choice.

An unpleasant thought came to him. He should have considered it before he ever set out. If Mentathos didn't want anyone going into the mine to look for silver, he had probably barricaded the entrance. Well, it was too late now. Having come this far he might as well see the thing through. With a gloomy sigh he rose to his feet and started up the ridge.

He was now on a spur of the main mountain. On its eastern side it fell away even more steeply than on the side he had climbed, flanking a deep and narrow valley with the next spur beyond. At the bottom a river tumbled over a series of rapids with the remains of an old rail track running beside it.

For a while he scrambled up the ridge, mainly on the Deniakis side of the actual crest, and only when the going became too difficult, moving a few paces over onto Mentathos land. Out there he felt exposed and vulnerable, almost on the skyline in this forbidden territory. The bleak, bare valley below seemed full of hidden watchers. He reached his goal with astonishing suddenness.

There was no mistaking it. This was Tartaros. There had to be a story about such a place. It was exactly as Aunt Nix had described it.

He had found his way blocked both sides of the ridge by an immense gash slicing into the spur, clean through the crest and into the southern slope, as if the mountain had been split apart by a single, unimaginably powerful stroke. Craning over the edge he saw that the two opposing cliffs reached almost down to the level of the valley floor. There were places where it seemed obvious that one cliff must once have fitted snugly against the other. And there, at the bottom of the opposite cliff and some way to his right, lay the entrance of Tartaros. It was simply a dark hole in the vertical rock. The rail track he had seen in the valley turned up into the cleft and turned again into the opening. He could see no sign of a barrier. That settled it. He would go on.

Easier said than done. Some of the rocks that composed the plunging slope were as large as a house, and he had to find ways either down or round them. And then, when he had almost reached the bottom, a secondary cliff forced him some way back along the valley before he could at last scramble down to the river.

He started warily up the rail track. The sleepers were mostly rotten and the rails were thick with rust, but in one place a swarm of flies buzzed around a pile of recent mule droppings—yesterday's, or the day's before, he thought. Alarming, but only half his mind was on the obvious dangers of what he was doing. The other half was trying to decide if what he was now seeing was at all like any of the shifting landscapes of his dream. Had one of them had a rail track running beside a river? Surely he would have remembered that, but no.

He came to the cleft and turned into it, left. It had been right in the dream, hadn't it? And of course no rail track. He'd been following Ridiki along a goat track. And those last dreadful moments, when he'd been toiling after her up the slope as she danced ahead . . . Here only a mild gradient led to the dark entrance of Tartaros.

He reached it and his heart sank. What he was looking at was no deeper than the cave on the way to Crow's Castle. Its back wall was formed by a solid-looking timber barrier. The rail track ran on through it beneath double doors with a heavy padlock hanging across the join.

Well, it would have to do. He would find somewhere to hide or bury the collar and pipes, and then call his second farewell through a crack in the door. Gloomily he entered the cave. It wasn't very promising. A natural cave might have had projections and fissures, but this had been shaped with stonecutters' tools to an even surface. A small cairn then, piled into one of the far corners . . .

Without any hope at all he checked the lock, and everything changed. It was locked sure enough, but only into one of the pair of shackles, one in each door, through which it was meant to run. Somebody must have deliberately left it like that, closing the door either from inside or outside in such a way that it looked from any distance as if it were properly fastened. For instance, they might have lost the key inside the mine. Or they might be inside now. Someone had been here not long ago. Those mule droppings . . . And the lock looked fairly new. Nothing like as old as the rails.

It didn't make any difference. He was still going to do what he'd come for. With a thumping heart he eased the door open, first just a crack, and then far enough for him to slip through.

Darkness. Silence, apart from the drumming of his own blood. No. From somewhere ahead the rustle of moving water. He waited, listening, before closing the door and taking his hand torch out of his satchel. Shading the light with his left hand, he switched it on. Cautiously he allowed a crack of light to seep between his fingers.

The rails stretched away into the dimness along a tunnel whose walls were partly natural, partly shaped with tools. Only a few paces along, low in the right-hand wall, he made out what he was looking for, a vertical crack in the rock, as wide as his clenched fist at the bottom and tapering to a point at about knee height. Having checked, and found it was deep enough, he laid the collar and pipes ready, collected some fragments of rock to seal them in with, knelt beside the crack, and picked up the collar, and straightened.

No need to shout. If Ridiki could hear him, it would not be with earthly ears, and suppose whoever had left the door unlocked was somewhere ahead down there, he would be nearer the source of the water-noises, which should be enough to mask a quiet call from the distance.

"Good-bye, Eurydice. Good-bye, Ridiki. Be happy where you are."

He was answered twice, first by the echo and then, drowning that out, by the bark of a dog, a sharp, triple yelp, a pause, and then the same again. And again. The alert call that every Deniakis dog was trained to give to attract its master's attention to something he might need to be aware of. It could have been Ridiki. (No, for course it couldn't. She was dead.) Out on the open hillside he would have known her voice from that of any other dog in Greece, but the echoing distances of the place muffled and changed it.

The call died away into uncertainty, as if the dog wasn't sure it was doing the right thing. Steff found he had sprung to his feet, tense with mixed terror and excitement. The pipes were still on the floor where he had left them. He stuffed the collar in his pocket and picked them up, but continued to stand there, strangely dazed. Whatever the risk, it was impossible to turn away. To do so would haunt him for the rest of his days. He had to be sure. Shielding the torch so that it lit only the patch of floor immediately in front of his feet, he stole on. The daze continued. He felt as if he carried some kind of shadow of himself inside himself, its hand inside the hands that held the pipes and torch, its heart beating to the beat of his heart, its feet walking with shadow feet inside his feet of flesh and bone but making a separate soft footfall.

And everything around him shared the same doubleness. In the world of flesh and bone this was simply an empty, worked-out silver mine that before that had been a deep cave. But, mine or cave, in the shadow world it was and always had been an entrance to the underworld. Along it, and all around him, invisible, imperceptible, flooded the souls of the freshly dead. And ahead of him there was a dog of flesh and bone who was also, somehow, the dog Cerberus, the dreadful three-headed guardian of that realm. And a nameless stream the shadow of whose waters was the River Styx. And, waiting for him on its further shore, Eurydice. Ridiki.

The daze faded abruptly. He was aware of some other change, but couldn't locate it. He stopped and stood listening. No, not a sound, a light, a faint orange glow from around a so-far unperceived bend in the tunnel. He moved on, step by cautious step. Even more slowly he edged round the bend. The water sounds became noticeably louder, telling him that they were made by something more than a trickle, more than a small stream. The source of light appeared, an ordinary oil lantern standing on a ledge carved into the opposite wall. Just beyond it, the dog.

A dog of the Deniakis breed, all right, though larger than most, almost twice the size of Ridiki, but very much her colouring. Its collar was fastened by a light chain to a shackle in the wall, and it was lying across the near side of the tunnel, with its head turned away from him, ears half pricked, motionless. He knew that pose only too well. It was waiting for the return of its master.

What now? In the world of flesh and bone the only sane thing would be to turn back. It was the pipes that made up his mind. Unconsciously while he hesitated he had been weighing them in his hand, but now he found himself gazing dreamily down at them. His shadow self returned, allowing him to look at them through shadow eyes, to see them for what they were in that dim light. In the world of fresh and blood he had brought them here as a tangible offering to make as part of his farewell to Ridiki, a way of telling himself that now, truly, finally, he was letting her go. But, like one of the echoes in this place of echoes, that purpose now reverberated back to him from the shadow world all changed, telling him that if he used them the pipes were a passport, a charm with which he might persuade the powers of the underworld to let him through.

Suppose it was all nonsense. Suppose the dog's only response was to set up a clamour of barking and bring its master running. The man must be a little way off, beyond the dog's awareness, to judge by its anxious, waiting pose. He'd have a good start. Once through the door he could run the collar through the lock-shackles and fasten it tight. It would take the man some while to force his way past that, and by then Steff would be out of the cleft and well up the hillside . . .

Before that half of his mind had finished these flesh-and-blood calculations his shadow self had moved him quietly out to the centre of the tunnel and put the pipes to his lips. He drew a calm breath and blew two sharp notes, well apart on the scale, three times repeated. All Deniakis dogs had been trained to the same signals, and since, once trained, they were going to be sold on, Nikos never allowed them to bond to a single man, but got them accustomed to obeying the commands of strangers. This was the *Attention* call, a musical version of the dog's *Alert*. Instantly the dog heaved itself onto its haunches. Its head swung round, ears pricked. Herd dogs have excellent sight, but Steff was some way from the lantern's dim light and the dog, he now saw, was old. Its movements had been stiff and there was something awkward about its posture, very like Ridiki's when she was at attention.

Nevertheless it recognised a stranger, and was about to spring up and rush yelling to the reach of its chain when Steff blew a long, fluttering call—*Down. Wait. Be Ready.*

The dog paused, uncertain. He blew the call again. The dog subsided, though still with obvious doubt, and lay with its muzzle on its outstretched forelegs. Its hackles continued to stir as he walked confidently forward, the pipes ready at his lips, but its training held. As he neared he saw why it had so reminded him of Ridiki. The left forepaw—what would have been the hand on a human arm—was missing as far as the wrist. Once well past the dog, he turned and played the first few notes of a local lullaby. *Relax.* It obeyed, obviously relieved, looking in fact rather pleased with itself at having performed a known task well. It was a nice old dog, he thought, not at all dreadful. And only one head.

And the same with everything else. The tunnel he was in was now an old mine shaft and nothing more. The dead no longer flooded invisibly along it—it was empty apart from himself. And what he was doing was once again pure, reasonless, dangerous folly. Only the memory of his earlier resolution carried him on.

Another lantern glowed in the distance. Very likely that was where the dog's master was doing whatever he was here for, but again the danger had to be faced. Twice now he had come to such a moment with nothing more to rely on than shadow certainties that he no longer felt, and twice they had compelled him to face the test. Why stop trusting them now? Still, spasms of fear shuddered through him as he stole nearer to the light, and he had to stop and wait for them to pass before he could force himself on.

Now he could see the end of the tunnel, a rock surface with a thick rope running across it through a series of old iron rings. The rail track curved round to the left, into the lantern light. The floor of the tunnel ended halfway across to the opposite wall—the gap must be the channel in which the water ran.

He edged along close to the left-hand wall, checking to the right on what he could see of that side of the chamber ahead, as more and more of it came into view. In fact it ended in a blank stone wall only a couple of paces round the corner. The water flowed out of it under a low arch.

At the tunnel's end, huddled close against the wall, he stood and listened, but the steady rustle of the water drowned any small sounds the man might be making, if he was there. Cautiously he peeped out, just far enough to see round the corner with one eye. The lantern stood on a flatbed rail trolley, a simple wooden platform on wheels, with a hinged handle either end for pushing or pulling. The rails ended a pace or two beyond it, and the chamber a little beyond that, with a blank wall through which the water flowed out of a tunnel high enough for man to stand in. The rope along the far wall continued through more rings and on into the tunnel.

At first there seemed to be no one about, but then a man's head and shoulders, facing away from Steff, rose from behind the trolley. For a moment he seemed to be standing in the river, but his body rocked as he lifted something heavy up onto the quayside, showing that he must be standing on some kind of boat or raft. The rope on the wall was for him to pull himself up and down the river.

Still with his back towards Steff he climbed up onto the quay and lifted his load onto the trolley and slid it forward. It was a sturdy wooden box, not large but obviously heavy. He returned to the raft and disappeared, clearly to fetch another one.

Steff had only a moment or two to think, but barely needed it. Everything he'd seen and been told seemed to click into place in his head. Somebody—probably one of the men who'd done the final survey on the mine and said it was worked out, had actually found a vein of fine silver, like what Alexander had used to pay his soldiers. He'd kept quiet about it until he could use it for himself. He'd then done a deal with Mentathos, to share the profits if he'd help. They had to keep dead quiet about it, because the silver really belonged to the mining company, and besides, if nobody knew, then they wouldn't have to pay taxes. (The papers were always full of this sort of shady dealings, and the men talked about them over their dinners.)

So what Steff was doing was no longer a silly escapade for which he'd be seriously punished if anyone found out. Suddenly it had become extremely dangerous. He'd better get out, and quick, while the man was busy and he still had time to pipe his way past the dog.

But the man was Charon the ferryman, and the river was the Styx, the first of the seven rivers of the underworld, and all around, at this very moment, unseen, unfelt, the dead were crowding the quay, begging for passage, paying him with the two coins that had been put in their mouths before they were buried.

There was some small change left from this week's pocket money. But how . . .?

Still hesitating, Steff edged an eye round the corner to check what he was doing. As it happened the man was looking straight towards the mouth of the tunnel.

He stared for an instant, and bellowed. Automatically Steff jerked back, caught his foot, and fell. Before he could rise the man was on him. He was grabbed by the shoulders, hauled to his feet, and shaken violently back and forth, while the man continued to bellow.

"Mother of Christ, who the hell are you? And what in God's name do you think you're doing here, you nosy little bastard? I'll show you!"

The man flung him back against the rock wall, grabbed him before he could fall, and began to batter him to and fro again.

"Charon?"

Winded, half-stunned, terrified, Steff wasn't aware of deciding to say the name. It was a barely audible croak, forced out of him by the violence of his shaking. But the man paused, staring. He wasn't much taller than Steff, but broad-shouldered, with a weather-beaten, flat, snub-nosed face and dark eyebrows that joined above his nose.

"Mother of Christ!" he said. "The boss sent you? That case, what cause you got to go sneaking around like that?"

"No . . . No . . . He didn't . . . No one did. I'm looking for Ridiki . . . My dog."

"So what the hell makes you think your bloody dog might be down here? Hector's the only dog down here. Come to that, how'd you get past him without him yelling his head off? And how come you know what the boss calls me?"

"She isn't down here—not like that. She's dead. A snake bit her. But Ridiki's short for Eurydice. That's her real name. The story, you see . . . And this is Tartaros. It's an entrance to the underworld . . ."

"And so I'm Charon. Look, kid, that was just a lucky guess. Like I said, it's what the boss calls me, one of his jokes, because of what the mine's called. Next thing you'll be telling me Hector's got three heads, and you charmed your way past him by playing him beautiful music."

"Well, sort of. I'd brought my pipes, you see, to leave for Ridiki, but when I saw he was one of our dogs, I played him . . ."

"Hold it there. One of your dogs? You're Deniakis? Don't tell me you're one of the old man's kids? No, they're older . . ."

"He's my uncle."

"Your dad was the one those bastards in Athens got?"

"That's right."

The man paused, thinking.

"Right," he said. "You're in a mess, kid, a bloody, stupid, dangerous mess you got yourself into. And by sheer fool's luck you've run into the only Mentathos who's going to get you out of it. Your dad was my wife's childhood sweetheart. All of ten years old they must have been. Fell for each other, *click!*, just like that. He smuggled a puppy down to show her, let her cuddle it. And they weren't supposed even to talk to each other; their dads would've flayed them if they'd heard, and they'd both got elder brothers at the school to keep them toeing the line. Year and a half they kept it up, stolen moments, couple of friends they could trust. Then her brother twigged, got up a Mentathos gang to take it out on your dad and his brother, but Deniakis—he's your uncle now—was waiting for us with his own gang, and between us we pretty well wrecked the school. Upshot was her dad took my wife away but they smuggled letters back and forth for years.

"She told me all this before we married—I didn't like it, of course—but she got me to understand she wasn't in love with him, not like that. He was going to come to our wedding in disguise, bringing his wife, but his ministry sent him to America, so when our first kid was on the way she wrote to him and asked him to be a sort of secret godfather. I'd tried to talk her out of it and I tried again when he wrote back and said he'd give us one of the Deniakis dogs. I could see the sort of trouble that would cause, but she was set on the idea so I cleared it with Mentathos. Not that he liked it either, but he owed me one. He's a hard man—hard as they come, but he pays his debts. Said OK, we could have the dog and told his men to let it alone.

"Someone didn't listen. You saw Hector's missing a foot. Fox trap, left deliberate. I caught the fellow that put it there. You'll know him if you meet him. Two fingers missing on his left hand, and he can count himself lucky I left him the hand . . ."

"Rania dropped a skillet on Ridiki's left leg—she didn't mean to, she's just clumsy, but it could've killed her."

"Right. Anyway, that's Hector. Best dog I ever owned, three legs or four. Took a bit of time for us to get him—Deniakis keeps count of his dogs. Your dad was dead by the time he came but a fellow called Nikos fixed it . . ."

"He helped me train Ridiki."

"Another thing we've got between us, then. Now, the fellows with the mules will be up here . . . let's see . . . bit over half an hour. Just time to get you clear."

"But . . . but I've got to see Dis about Ridiki."

"Listen, kid . . . what's your name?"

"Steff."

"All right, Steff. Looking at it your way, if Hector's Cerberus and I'm Charon, then Dis is the boss down here. You absolutely do not want to see Dis. River in the underworld—isn't that right?—fall into it and you forget everything. Same here. Fall into our river and next time anyone sees you you've forgotten everything all right, because you've been washed up in Siren's Bay with a hole in your head might have been got by you banging it on a rock. Or maybe being banged with a rock. No, I wouldn't put it past him. Why d'you think I beat you up the way I did? Sorry about that, but I couldn't let you go, not after what you'd seen, and I was scared rigid what he'd do when he got his hands on you. You won't get any sympathy out of him—you'd just as well ask old Hector . . . Wait! That's it, Steff lad. What call d'you think Dis has to be interested in dogs? Cerberus is the one you've got to ask. You can do that as you're going."

"But . . ."

"You've got two choices, Steff. Either you do what I tell you, ask Hector for what you want, and then make yourself scarce, or I carry you kicking and screaming out onto the hillside and tie you up and come back for you later. Either way I'm taking a hell of a risk, trusting you not letting on to anyone. OK, your uncle would flay you if he found out, same as my wife would flay me if she found out I'd handed you over to the boss. But your uncle's not the only one. You're telling nobody. Got it? Nobody. Now, make up your mind."

Steff shook his head. He couldn't think. The man was too much for him, not just too big and too strong, but too full of adult energy and command.

"All right," he muttered.

The man grunted and picked up his lantern.

They walked up the tunnel, side by side. Hector came in sight, lying as Steff had first seen him, but with his ears fully pricked at the sound of his master's returning footfall. The man checked his watch again.

"Still got time for it. Just like to see Hector doing his tricks after all these years. I'll have to tell Maria about you, any case, and I'll lay she'll be wanting to meet you. Ready? Pipe away, then."

They halted. Half heartedly Steff put the pipes to his lips. They were Ridiki's. He'd never expected to use them again. The sharp notes of the *alert* sounded along the tunnel. Hector rose, puzzled for a moment, but then eagerly, as if glad to perform for his master.

"Well, I'll be busted!" said the man, laughing aloud as Hector responded to the next two calls. "Ten years and more it's got to be since he last did that. I've never had call to learn the signals. Well done, old boy. Now sit. Steff's got something to ask you."

Obediently Hector rose again to his haunches. Steff knelt to bring their two heads level. He took Ridiki's collar from his pocket and held it forward. Hector gave it an investigating sniff and then smelt it carefully over. To a dog, another dog's smell is its name.

He would know Ridiki if he met her. Only he wouldn't—she was dead.

When he'd sniffed enough, Steff leaned back to ease his posture. The movement caused the shadows on the wall to shift, as the two shadows of Steff's head, one thrown by the lantern in the man's hand and the other by the lantern on the opposite wall, detached themselves from Hector's shadow, so that it now seemed as if the shadows of three heads rose from the shapeless mass of overlapping shadows cast by the two bodies.

The shadow world had returned in all its strange certainty, and Steff knew that he now spoke through Hector to his shadow self, the monstrous guardian of the underworld.

"Oh, Cerberus, please . . ." he whispered. "Please can you let Ridiki come back home with me? . . . I don't expect you can, but . . . anyway, please look after her. Thank you."

He rose, and his two shadows now hid the dog's and the shape on the wall meant nothing. He wiped his eyes on his sleeve, and when he looked again he saw, towering over his own double shadow, the single shadow of the man, cast by the lamp on the opposite wall. The lamp the man was carrying shone directly on the wall, making his shadow almost too faint to see, but it was there, reaching up to the tunnel roof and arching over them because the man was standing closer to the light source.

"You know you mustn't look round until you are out?" said the man, amused but sympathetic.

An echo floated back, toneless, a shadow voice, whispering out of the rock of Tartaros.

". . . until you are out."

"Yes, I know," said Steff. "Thank you. I'll go now. I'll turn left at the river and try and climb up that way. Then I won't run into your friends with the mules."

"Easier that way, any case," said the man. "There's a bit of a track. And look. Wednesdays Mentathos runs a truck down to the town, so the women can do their shop. I'll be waiting for you after school. Don't let on you know me—neither of us wants anyone asking questions—just follow where I go and I'll take you to meet Sophie. Better tell someone you'll be late home. OK?"

"OK. See you," said Steff, and turned away into the unceasing stream of the invisible dead moving in the other direction. The lantern glow dwindled behind him. Reluctantly he switched on his hand torch. Its sharp, white, modern beam banished the shadow world. The tide of dead ceased to exist, a remembered delusion. None of that had been true. He'd taken a crazy risk for a silly, childish hope, and been extraordinarily lucky. Ridiki was dead, buried under the fig tree.

And yet she was there, trotting silently behind him. He'd always been able to tell, just as he could tell exactly where his hand was if he closed his eyes and moved it around.

Oh, nonsense! Kidding himself again, the way he'd been kidding himself all through the adventure because he so longed for it to be true. All he was doing was making it worse for himself every step he took until he reached the open air and turned round and she wasn't there. Torturing himself with hope. Grow up, Steff. Get it over.

No, he told himself. This was another test, the hardest of all.

Somehow it was now far further up the dark and empty tunnel than it had been when he'd been stealing so cautiously in, and all that way he fought the compulsion, grimly forcing himself into the gale of the rational world as it blew every shred of its shadow counterpart away. All he had left of it was this one last tatter, that when he at last looked back and saw nothing but the rock-rubble floor of the cleft he would still at least know that he had kept faith with Ridiki.

He reached the wooden barrier, opened the door, closed his eyes and held it for long enough for her to slip through before he shut it. Still with closed eyes he set his shoulders against the barrier to check his direction and purposefully walked the few paces more to bring himself clear of the cave before he opened them.

There was no need to look round. She had slipped past him and was already there, waiting for him in the last of daylight.

Ridiki, eyes bright, ears cocked, tail high, delighted to see him. She was wearing her Sunday collar. He dropped to his knees and held out his arms. She pranced towards him, but stopped just out of reach. He shuffled forward and she drew away. Her ears twitched back a little and hackles stirred—not a threat but a warning. There were no footprints in the patch of dust where she'd been standing

"I mustn't touch you . . .?" he whispered.

Her ears pricked, her hackles smoothed, and the look of anxiety left her eyes.

"Can you come home with me—part of the way at least? The man—Charon, I call him—says I've got to get out before the men come with the mules. I suppose they move the silver after dark."

He'd always talked to her when they were alone together, telling her his thoughts, explaining what he was up to. He didn't expect her to understand, but now for answer she turned and trotted off down the cleft. He followed. At the river she turned confidently to the left, but stayed on the track further than he'd have done. But she seemed to know what she was doing. This was a much easier climb than the route he'd taken down would have been, and towards the top they slanted to the left and so reached the crest of the ridge very close to where Steff had started down, but on the other side of the cleft.

The moon was rising, near to the full. He was interested to see that Ridiki cast a shadow, dark and definite enough, though somehow less so than the hard-edged black shadows of the rocks around. The shadow of a shadow, so to speak, for she herself was a shadow, a shadow somehow made solid. For him at least. He wondered whether anyone else would be able to see her.

As soon as they started down the moon was hidden by the mass of the ridge behind them, but Ridiki still seemed able to find the way. He could just pick out her yellow rump as she led him down twisting animal tracks till they came out on one of the many shepherds' trails that crisscrossed the mountainside. From here on he knew the way, and without being told she dropped back to her usual place close behind him with her muzzle level with his left knee.

His heart lightened. So she hadn't just been making sure he reached a point from which he could get safely home. She was coming with him.

Tired though his body was he strode home so happy that he barely noticed the journey. Even then it was well after midnight when he scratched on Papa Alexi's shutter. The old man must have been sitting up waiting for him. He opened the door almost at once, a pale, stooped figure in his long nightshirt.

"Not bad," he said. "I thought you'd be later. Get done what you wanted?"

"Yes. I was very lucky. It was all right. You didn't tell anyone?"

"Waiting till morning. Good night, then."

"Good night. And thank you very much."

Over the next weeks he slowly became used to Ridiki's strange existence, learning to think of her as his dog, there, real, as she always had been, though no one else on the farm could see her. Nor could any of the other dogs, though old Hera, stone deaf and almost blind, sniffed interestedly at her when she greeted her and thumped her scabby tail on the ground. She knew. Ridiki seemed to mind about the dogs not seeing her far more than she did about the people, and made a point of visiting her every day.

Invisibility had its advantages. She could now come indoors, and slept weightless at the foot of Steff's bed. She trotted down to school with him and curled up under his bench or found safe corners to lie in so that she could still be nearby while he was doing stuff with his friends. At first he'd been worried about what might happen if someone happened to walk into her or trod on her, but she was careful not let it happen. As the days went by he came to realise that all the time she was with him she was performing an extremely difficult feat, a balancing act on a precarious rope bridge between the world of shadows and the world of flesh and blood. Any sudden jolt might toss her down into the nowhere between those worlds, any extra strain might unravel the fastening at one end or the other. A touch from his hand would do it.

So mostly she behaved as any other dog would have done. He had trained her not to eat anything except from his hand or from her bowl, but he had no shadow food to give her so she fended for herself, stalking shadow mice around the farm, or pouncing on small shadow creatures among the tussocks beside a path, or finding shadow scraps behind the kitchen door. Once, down on the shore, she dragged out something heavy from between two rocks and lay in a patch of shade holding one end of the invisible object between her forepaws and growling contentedly as she gnawed at the other end. She drank from a shadow stream that seemed to run down the far side of orchard. Steff asked Papa Alexi whether there'd ever been a stream there, and he said yes, but it had been diverted fifty years ago to water the fruit terraces. She peed and shat like a normal dog. Her faeces glistened a little while in the sun, but before they'd begun to dry and darken they faded into the ground.

She came with Steff when the man he thought of as Charon took him to meet his wife, Sophie, in a dark little bar in a backstreet, where none of the Deniakis or Mentathos people were likely to see them together. Charon fetched food and drink, but just had a glass of beer and left.

"Isn't this wonderful!" said Sophie as soon as he'd gone. "Secret meetings again! And you look just like him, that age! My heart stopped when I saw you."

They talked about Steff's father—she told him a lot he didn't know—and then about Steff himself, and his mother and his other family—she seemed to want to know everything—until it was time for her to catch the Mentathos truck home.

"Same again next week?" she said as she rose.

"Oh . . . Yes, please. If you like."

It became a pattern for the next few weeks. She was like the cheerful and understanding aunt he'd never had. He didn't know what she got out of it, but she obviously enjoyed their meetings. He told Papa Alexi and Aunt Nix about them, knowing they wouldn't pass it on, but he didn't expect anyone else at the farm to notice that he was getting back late on Wednesdays. He was wrong.

It wasn't even a Wednesday. He got home at his usual time, just as the informal mid-day meal on the vine-shaded terrace was breaking up for everyone to go and have their afternoon rest. He was greeted by a shout from Mitsos.

"Hey, Steff. Where'd you get to yesterday? Not the first time, neither. Meeting some girl, I bet, down in the town. Tell us about her. Plump little piece, just coming ripe? You lucky little sod!"

Being Mitsos, he was aiming for maximum embarrassment, and a couple of months back he'd have got it. But thanks to Tartaros, and Ridiki's return, and most of all to his meetings with Sophie, something had changed inside Steff. A joke Sophie had made to Charon a couple of weeks back even told him how to answer.

He picked up a chunk of bread, bit off a corner, chewed, and tucked it into his cheek.

"Dead wrong, Mitsos," he said. "She's a married woman."

He chewed a bit more and added, ". . . and her husband isn't jealous."

Everyone laughed, partly at the joke, partly at Mitsos, but mainly with surprise at quiet, withdrawn, anxious Steff coming up with something like that. His uncle caught his eye and gave a nodded of approval—he thought boys should be able to stand up for themselves. Even so, it was a surprise when he returned after everyone else was gone, and Steff was finishing his meal, with Ridiki curled on the paving beside him. Steff rose. His uncle gestured to him to sit, did so himself, and picked up an olive.

"Got over losing that dog of yours?" he asked.

Out of the corner of his eye Steff saw Ridiki look up, amused.

"Just about," he said. "I missed her a lot at first."

"Hurts a bit every time, and the first one's worst. Ready for another one, d'you think? Atalanta's litter's ready to look at. Got a chap coming tomorrow to choose one, but you get first pick."

"Oh, but . . . I thought they'd all be spoken for."

"You're family. I'd give you one myself, but your mother's sent the money. She wants it from her."

Steff bent as if to scratch his ankle while he thought, letting him look directly at Ridiki for help. Her ears were pricked with interest and her eyes amused.

He straightened.

"Thank you very much," he said. "I'll go and look at them when Nikos's finished his rest."

As he watched his uncle walk away it struck him that he hadn't seen Ridiki looking that lively for quite some time. Over the last few weeks she'd been spending more and more of her time asleep, and when she was awake her interest in everything around her was somehow less intense than it used to be. He'd started to wonder whether she was tired because it was becoming more of an effort for to maintain the between-two-worlds balance she needed for these spells of wakefulness.

Did she think another dog would be company for her, liven her up? Or for him, and allow her to go back into the shadows where she belonged?

❧

Though she knew Steff well, Atalanta was a jealous mother, and Nikos had to hold her while Steff picked the pups out of the box one by one, turned them over to check their sex, and set them on the floor of the kennel-shed as if to see how they reacted while Ridiki looked and sniffed them over. Their eyes were open but still blurred, and the black markings they would have as adults only just visible as darker patches fawn birth-fur. The first three were bitches. They looked lost and miserable and headed straight back to the box with the rubber-legged waddle of small pups.

The fourth was a dog. He stood his ground, peering around with an absurd expression of eager bewilderment. Steff held out a hand. The pup sniffed at it, gave it an experimental lick, and sucked hopefully at a fingertip. When the hand was withdrawn he continued sniffing, to Nikos's eyes at empty air, and then attempted to lick something, reaching so far that he almost tumbled on his face as Ridiki withdrew her invisible nose.

But not invisible to the puppy.

"Seen a ghost," said Nikos, laughing. "You get that with some dogs. Hera, now, and she's his—let's see—great-grandmother."

"Can I have him?" said Steff. "I don't want another bitch, not so soon after Ridiki."

"Good choice. You've the makings of a sound dog there. Mind you, he'll look a bit like something out of a circus, those markings. There's some wouldn't want that."

Steff hadn't paid much attention to the markings, merely registering that the dog would be mainly the Deniakis golden-yellow, with a few black bits. Now he saw that these patches, still no more than a light golden-orange, were going to darken into five almost perfect circles, three on the left flank and two on the right, like a clown's horse in a picture book. He was a comical little scrap.

"What can I call him?" he asked. "Did the old Greeks have clowns?"

"Yes, you've got a problem there—not a lot of fun, that lot. Hold it. There was that fellow wrote a play about frogs. Aristo something. Aristotle?"

"I'll ask Papa Alexi. I could call him Risto."

Three months later came the start of the grape harvest. School was over for the next few weeks, so Steff helped all morning in the vineyard—a cheerful time, with a lot of laughter and chat between the regular farmhands and the casual pickers from the town. But it was clearly going to be a hot and tiring afternoon, and he'd not been looking forward to it when, just as everyone was rousing themselves from the midday break, Nikos said "They've more than enough hands here, Steff. They won't miss two of us. Like to show me how that dog of yours is getting on?"

This was part of the deal. Not wanting to see a good dog spoiled, Nikos had been a bit reluctant to let Steff train Risto on his own, but he'd agreed to let him do the first stages, learning the simple pipe calls and so on, and see then to see how it had gone. Risto was still more puppy than dog, and still a bit of a clown, but he was a quick and eager learner, and had Ridiki to show him what was expected of him.

He was also a show-off—part of his clownishness—and in the dogs' eyes Nikos was the leader of the human pack, and so he really laid it on for him, quivering with excitement as he sat waiting for the last note of each call and then darting into action. He finished with a theatrically stealthy stalk of a rock with a sheepskin draped across it, moving left and right, crouching and moving on, exactly on each call.

Nikos laughed aloud.

"Pretty good," he said. "He's got the instinct in him, and then some. Never seen a pup that far on. Like to try him on a few live ones?"

He whistled for his own dog, Ajax, and led the way up to the rough pastures above the vineyards. Risto watched, thrilled and eager, while Ajax cut out three staid old ewes who knew what was expected of them almost as well as he did. Then, at first with Ridiki to guide him but soon on his own, he raced off to team up with Ajax and move the patient sheep across the slope, between two large boulders, round and back before releasing them. He returned panting, delighted with his own achievement, lapping up all the praise Steff could give him.

"Don't overdo that," said Nikos. "He's big-headed enough for three dogs already. Pretty good, mind you—good as I've seen. I'll tell your uncle you're doing fine. That's enough for now. He's only a pup still, and he's all in. Not worth going back to the vineyard. Give yourselves a break."

So Steff went back to the farm house and settled on a rock in the shade below the terrace to begin his weekly letter to his mother, with Ridiki and Risto curled up either side of him. The evenings were earlier now and the sky was just starting to redden as he gazed out over immense distances of the coastline beneath the sinking sun. Above him on the terrace some of the women were getting things ready for the party Deniakis held every year to celebrate the start of the grape picking. A happy and peaceful evening, but at the same time full of the feel of coming change, of the world readying itself for winter. The bustle on the terrace increased. The first of the workers began to arrive. Risto woke.

Puppy fashion, he'd forgotten his weariness, couldn't imagine such a state was possible for him. He looked up at Steff. Not a hope. But there was Ridiki beyond him, still asleep. He pranced round, springy with pent energy, crouched an inch from her nose and snorted. She opened an eye, raised her head and yawned. He rose onto his hind legs and pawed the air. Ridiki looked at Steff—if she'd have been human she'd have shrugged resignedly, Kids!—and she was off, streaking away down the slope into the orchard, jinking in and out between the trees, with Risto after her, sometimes on her tail, sometimes careering on after one of her sudden full-speed turns, braking so frenziedly that at one point he went tumbling head over heels, and then racing to make up the lost ground.

At that speed they couldn't keep it up for more than a few minutes and then came back side to side to Steff and sat panting, tongues lolling out, but still bright-eyed with the fun of what they'd been doing. Somebody coughed overhead and he looked up.

It was his uncle's new wife, Maria, holding her baby perched on the terrace wall to watch Risto racing around the orchard. There were people who said her mother was a witch and had put a spell on Deniakis to make him fall for someone who wasn't that young or that pretty, or rich enough to bring him that much of a dowry. But Aunt Nix had told Steff this was nonsense, and they'd been lovers for several years.

At Steff's movement she looked down.

"Playing hunt-puppy all on his own," she said. "Times I'd almost have sworn I could see the other dog."

His hair prickled on his nape.

"Oh . . . Well, he's Hera's great-grandson," he managed. "Nikos says she used to see ghosts sometimes."

Automatically Maria flicked her fingers to keep the ghost clear of her baby. Steff looked down anxiously at Ridiki. Her whole attitude had changed, become quietly solemn. Faintly through her body he could see the shapes of the grass-stems she was lying on.

Steff nodded and rose. He was ready. Everything seemed to have been telling him that this was the moment. With Risto at his heels he followed her along below the terrace wall, up round the main farmhouse and between the sheds and barns to the fig tree beside the gate. The lower branches had drooped down to fill the gap he'd made when he'd dug her grave, but she snaked in beneath them and curled herself up in the place her flesh-and-bone remains lay arm's-length down. He knelt and reached in towards her, but from habit withheld his hand just before he reached her. She raised her head and looked him in the eyes.

"Good-bye, Ridiki," he said for the third time. "Good-bye, Eurydice."

For a moment he thought he felt the feathery touch of her tongue on the back of his fingers, but then Risto, nosing in beside him, licked her firmly on the muzzle and she melted into the ground.

For a little longer Steff stayed where he was, kneeling by Ridiki's grave, quietly letting her go. Then he rose and walked slowly back towards the sounds of the party, knowing that he would remember her all his life, but no longer, now, with grief.

# Wizand

## Foreword

THE CLOSEST ANALOGY THAT I can find in the material world for the behaviour of a wizand is that of certain tropical ticks, though the similarity applies only to one part of the life cycle. These ticks hatch from eggs, go through a larval stage, pupate, emerge as adults, and mate. The male then dies. Nothing like this occurs with a wizand.

Having mated, however, the female tick climbs a grass stem or bush to a suitable height, tenses her limbs to spring, and locks the joints so that the tension is maintained with no further effort on her part. She then goes into a state that cannot be called life, since there are no metabolic processes, but is not death either. It is not known how long she can maintain this condition, but an instance of nine years is recorded.

At length the necessary stimulus—a warm-blooded animal—comes within range of her senses. Her joints unlock. The released tension hurls her forward, and if all goes well she lands on the creature's hide, clutches with powerful claws and sinks her modified mouth structure into the skin.

She distends her body with blood—her one meal as an adult tick—and this provides her with sufficient protein to form her eggs and lay them before she too dies.

Wizands are asexual, so they do not exactly mate or reproduce. They are technically immortal, but since both of their host organisms are mortal they may perish if they fail to make the transfer to the alternate host before the previous one dies. They do not reproduce in any normal sense, but they might be considered fissiparous, since, on the rare occasions when lightning strikes an ash tree inhabited by a wizand, the wizand is likely to divide into two or more entities. This is not an event that a wizand would in any way welcome, since it involves a proportional division of power between the resulting lesser wizands, but in the old days it used to be just enough to maintain the population.

Wizands, of course, were always scarce and local, and modern forestry methods—the reduction of woodland, the decline of coppicing, and the introduction of machinery to grub out the roots of felled trees—have reduced their numbers to a point where there are probably not more than half a dozen of them left in the whole of Europe, and because of the very different life expectancy of the two hosts only one or two of these is likely to be in the active phase at any particular time.

## Phase A

One afternoon, late in October 1679, Phyllida Blackett sat by her hearth. Her kettle hissed on the hub. A log flared and flared again, though it had been two years drying in the shed. But Phyllida sat placidly stroking the cat on her lap as if this were an evening like any other.

As it began to grow dark she took the new broom she had cut and bound—ash handle and birch twigs—and propped it behind the door. She picked up her old broom, carried it out into the wood that surrounded her cottage, and slipped it into the hollow centre of an old ash tree.

"You bide there and take your rest," she said. "And luck befall you next time. I'd see to that, did I know how."

She was a thoughtful symbiote.

Later that night, as she had known they would—known from the hiss of the kettle, the flames spurting from the log, the grain of the cat's fur—the Community of the Elect came up the hill and laid hands on her. While their minister chanted psalms in the belief that he was restraining her powers, they drove a stake into the ground, piled logs from her shed around it, and bound her to the stake with cords that had been nine days soaking in the holy water of their font. Before they fired the wood they searched her cottage, found the broomstick behind the door, and added it to the pile, but not, of course, within her reach.

A wizand has no ears, so the one in the old broomstick could not be said to have heard Phyllida's screams, but it sensed them, as it sensed the yells and jeering of the Community, ringing the bonfire. But unlike the exulting mob it knew that the screams were not of agony. Phyllida had both power and knowledge. She had seen to it that she would feel no pain. She could, if she had chosen, have lived longer, either by moving to a different district or by using their joint power and knowledge, hers and the wizand's, to defend her cottage. But she felt that the time was ripe. It was better to go cleanly like this than to have the Community eventually take her in her helpless senility. The wizand, of course, for its very different reasons, took the same view.

Still, Phyllida screamed. She could just have well have simply chanted the words that she wove into the screams, but then her jeering captors might have begun to doubt that they were in full control, and themselves fallen silent, and been afraid. Better to harness the anger and frustration and cruelty that streamed out of them as they watched her burn, to add that power to her own, to use it to bind their souls to this place after they died, to hold them back from both heaven and hell and fasten them to the sour clods and granite of this valley for three hundred years and thirty and three more.

Enormous energies were released by this final exercise of power. As they finished their work the wizand absorbed them into itself. At last, when the screams were silent, the Community trooped back down to their village in a single compact body, moving like sleepwalkers, and the wizand, sated, slipped out of the broomstick into the ash tree itself, found a place close above the bole where it was both safe and comfortable, and let itself drift into torpor.

Eighty odd years later a young and energetic man inherited the estate. He looked at the abandoned village at the foot of the hill, disliked its aspect, and gave orders for a fresh settlement to be built further down the stream. To provide an economic basis for the villagers he set about a general improvement of the land, the enclosure of fertile areas, and the exploitation of timber resources. Men came to coppice the wood.

As the first axe bit ringingly into the ash tree the wizand woke and glided down into the base of the bole, just below ground level. Next spring a ring of young shoots sprang from the still-living sapwood beneath the bark. They grew to wands, then poles. When they were an inch or so thick the wizand slid back up into one and waited again.

Seven times, at twenty-year intervals, the wood was fresh coppiced, but only for two or three years in each cycle were the saplings right for the wizand's needs, and no possible host came near while that was so. By the time the timber was carted away it was long poles, thicker than a man's calf, and the wizand, safe in the bole, waited without impatience for the next regrowth.

The economics of forestry changed again, and the coppicing ceased. It was another hundred and ten years before the ash tree was once more felled. This time it happened with the clamour of an engine, and hooked teeth on a chain that clawed so fast into the trunk that the wizand needed to wake almost fully from its torpor and hurry past before it was trapped above the cut. More engines dragged the timber away, and the shattered wood was left in peace. Next spring, as always, fresh shoots sprang up, ringing the severed bole.

## Phase B

A man's voice.

"These look about the right size. Which one do you want, darling?"

Another voice, petulant with boredom.

"I don't know."

The second voice triggered the change. Instantly the wizand was fully alert, waiting, knowing its own needs, just as a returning salmon knows the stream that spawned it. It guided the reaching arm. Through the young bark of the sapling it welcomed palm and fingers. The hand was very small, a child's, about seven years old, but now that the wizand was properly awake it saw how time was running out. There was little chance of another possible host coming by, and none of the ash tree being coppiced again, before the appointed hour.

"This one," said the child's voice, firmly.

A light saw bit sweetly in. The wizand stayed above the cut.

"I'll carry it," said the child.

"If you like. Just don't get it between your legs. Or mine. Now what we want next is a birch tree, and some good hemp cord. None of your nasty nylon—not for a witch's broom."

When the children came in from their trick-or-treating the several witches piled their brooms together. As they were leaving, a child happened to pick out the wrong one. She let go and snatched her hand back with a yelp.

"It bit me," she said, and started to cry, more frightened than hurt.

"Of course it did," said Sophie Winner. "That's my broom. It won't let anyone else touch it."

They thought she was joking, of course, and later that evening Simon and Joanne Winner found it gratifying that Sophie was so pleased with her new broom that she took it up to bed with her, and went upstairs without any of the usual sulkings and dallyings.

Sophie dreamed that night about flying. It was a dream she'd had before, so often that she thought she'd been born with it.

The wizand was always cautious with a fresh symbiote. The revelation, when it came, was likely to be a double shock, with the discovery both of the wizand's existence, and of the symbiote's true self. But hitherto the girl had always been around puberty. It had never dealt with a child as young as Sophie, with her preconceptions unhardened. If anything, it was she who surprised the wizand.

A fortnight after Halloween she took her broom into the back garden, saying that she was going to sweep the leaves off the lawn.

"If you like," said her father, laughing. "They'll blow around a bit in this wind, but give it a go."

He went to fetch his video camera.

The wizand could have swept the lawn on its own, but with her parents watching through the patio window Sophie kept firm hold of it, following its movements like a dancing partner, while it used the wind to gather the leaves into three neat piles in places where they would no longer blow around.

"It's wonderful what a kid can do by way of work, provided she thinks she's playing," said her father. He was the sort of parent that hides from himself the knowledge that his relationship with his own child is not what it should be by theorising about the behaviour of children in general.

When she'd finished, Sophie went up to her room and sat cross-legged and straight-backed in the middle of the floor, with the broom across her thighs and her hands grasping the stick at either end. She waited.

"Yes?" said the wizand.

Sophie heard the toneless syllable as clearly as if it had been spoken aloud, but knew that it hadn't come to her through her ears. She answered in the same manner, inside her head.

"I knew you were there. The moment I touched the tree. I felt you."

"Ycs."

"What are you? A demon or something?"

"Wizand."

Sophie accepted the unfamiliar word without query.

"Am I a witch?"

"Yes."

"I thought so. Can we fly?"

"Yes."

"We'd need to be invisible."

"No."

"But . . . Oh, you mean you can't do that? Couldn't I?"

"Not yet."

"You can fly, and you can sweep. Anything else?"

"Power."

"Oh . . ."

"Not yet."

Sophie felt relieved. She didn't know why.

"We'd better wait for a dark night," she said.

Sophie chose a Friday, so that she could lie in on Saturday morning. She went to bed early and waited for her parents to come in and say goodnight. As soon as the door closed behind them she fetched her broom from the corner beside the wardrobe.

"They won't come back," she told it. "Let's go."

"Sleep," said the wizand.

"Oh. It won't be just dreaming again? We're really going to do it?"

"Yes."

Sophie climbed into bed with the broom on the duvet beside her, closed her eyes and was instantly asleep. The wizand waited until it sensed that the parents were also sleeping, then woke her by sending a trembling warm sensation into her forearm where it lay against the ash wood. She sat up, fully aware.

"Can we get through the window, or do we have to go outside?" she asked. "I'd need to turn off the burglar alarm."

"Window."

She pushed the sash up as far as it would go and picked up the broom again.

"Naked," said the wizand.

"Oh, all right."

Her parents considered Sophie a prudish child, but she unhesitatingly stripped off her nightie. As soon as she touched the broom again her body knew what to do. Both hands gripped the handle near the tip. She straddled the stick, as if it had been a hobby horse, and laid herself close along it, with the smooth wood pressing into chest and belly. A word came into her mouth that she had never before spoken. She said it aloud, and as the broom moved softly forward and upward she hooked her right ankle over her left beneath the bunched birch twigs. Together they glided cleanly through the window and into the open.

It was a chilly February night, with a heavy cloud layer releasing patches of light drizzle, but Sophie felt no cold. Indeed her body seemed to be filling with a tingling warmth, and as their speed increased the rush of the night air over her skin was a delectable coolness around that inward glow. Flying was like all the wonderful moments Sophie had ever known, but better, realer, truer. This was what she was for. Thinking about it beforehand she had imagined that the best part would be looking down from above on familiar landmarks, school and parks and churches small and strange-angled beneath her; but now, absorbed in the ecstasy of the thing itself, she barely noticed any of that until the lit streets disappeared behind her and they were flying low above darkened fields, almost skimming the hedgerow trees.

The broomstick swerved suddenly aside, and up, curving away, and then curving again and flying far more slowly.

"What?" it asked.

Sophie peered ahead and saw a skeletal structure against the glow from the motorway service station.

"Pylons," she said. "Dad says they carry electricity around."

The broomstick flew along the line of the wires, keeping well clear of them, then circled for height and crossed them with plenty of room to spare. Beyond them it descended and skimmed on westward, rising again to cross the motorway as it headed for the now looming hills.

It rose effortlessly to climb them, crossed the first ridge and dipped into a deep-shadowed valley. Halfway down the slope it slowed, circled over a dark patch of woodland, and settled down into a clearing among the trees. The moment Sophie's bare feet touched earth the broom became inert. If she'd let go of it, it would have fallen to the ground.

She stood and looked around her. It was almost as dark in the clearing as it was beneath the trees, though they were mostly leafless by now. An owl was hooting a little way down the hill. Sophie had never liked the dark, even in the safety of her own bedroom, but she didn't feel afraid.

"Can I make light?" she said.

"Hand. Up," said the wizand.

Again her body knew what to do. She raised her right arm above her head, with the wrist bent and the fingers loosely cupped around the palm. Something flowed gently out of the ashwood into the hand that held it, up that arm, across her shoulder blades, on up her raised arm, and into the hand. A pale light glowed between her fingers, slightly cooler than the night air, something like moonlight but with a mauvish tinge, not fierce but strong enough to be reflected from tree trunks deep in the wood.

There was nothing special about the clearing. It was roughly circular, grassy, with a low mound to one side. A track ran across in front of the mound. It didn't look as if it was used much. That was all. But the clearing spoke to her, spoke with voices that she couldn't hear and shapes that she couldn't see. There was a pressure around her, and a thin, high humming, not reaching her through her ears but sounding inside her head, in the same way that the wizand spoke to her. She wasn't afraid, but she didn't like it. She wasn't ready.

"Let's go home," she said.

"Yes," said the wizand.

On the way back the rapture of flight overcame her once more, but this time there was a small part of her that held itself back, so that she was able to think about what was happening to her. It was then that she first began to comprehend something central to her nature, when she saw that the rapture arose not directly from the flying itself, but from the ability to fly, the power. That was what the wizand had meant, when it had first spoken to her. Power.

Sophie was an intelligent and perceptive child, but hitherto, like most children, she had taken her parents for granted. They were what they were, and there was no need for her to wonder why. The coming of the wizand changed that, because of the need to conceal its existence from them. This meant that Sophie had to think about them, how to handle them, how to make sure they got enough of her to satisfy them, so that they didn't demand anything she wasn't prepared to give. Soon she understood them a good deal better than they did her, and realised—as they didn't, and never would—that there was no way in which she and they could ever be fully at ease with each other. It wasn't lack of love on their part, or at least what they thought of as love, but it was the wrong sort of love, too involved, to eager to share in all that happened to her, to rejoice in her happinesses and grieve for her miseries. It was, she saw, a way of owning her. She could not allow that.

Obviously this wasn't anything she could explain to them, but just as obviously it would be no use her shutting herself up in her room for hours, alone with her broom. She mustn't even make a particular fuss of it—no more fantastic feats of leaf-sweeping—so she wrote a label for it, "Sophie's Broom. Do not touch," and propped it into the corner behind the wardrobe. She made a point of being around whenever she guessed her parents would like her to be, so that they'd be less likely to come looking for her at other times. To minimise intrusions in her absence she started to keep her room clean and neat, and to fold her clothes and put them away.

Her moodswings became less marked, and she went to bed at the right time without making a fuss—or mostly so, because sometimes she'd throw a minor tantrum, enjoying it in a rather cold-blooded way, so that they wouldn't start to feel that they no longer had the daughter they were used to. So family tensions eased, and life became more comfortable for all three of them. Her parents, of course, believed that this was their doing, and congratulated themselves on their patient handling of her.

They were delighted, too, by her sudden hunger for books. She had been slow to start reading, but now caught up rapidly with her age group and overtook most of them. It barely mattered what the book was about. Anything satisfied the hunger, at least momentarily, and then it was back, strong as ever.

"I suppose witches have to read a lot, to learn how to do stuff."

"Yes."

"The trouble is, there don't seem to be that sort of books any more. And there aren't any witches to teach me, either. I mean, not my sort. There are those ones on TV who dance in circles and do chants to the Earth Mother, but that's different."

"Yes."

"I suppose what you're used to is someone like me going to grown-up witches to learn stuff."

"Yes."

"Well, there aren't any. Not anymore. You'd feel them, wouldn't you? Anyway, I would. I don't know how I would, but I would."

"Yes."

What the wizand in fact sensed was a change far more profound than the mere absence of active symbiotes, and more profound too than the obvious physical changes—the chain saw that had felled the ash tree, the huge contraptions that could fly far higher and faster than any broomstick, the flameless warmth in the houses, the night-time glow over the cities—those were superficial. The major change was in people's minds, their hopes, fears, understandings, beliefs, disbeliefs. The people who had burnt Phyllida Blackett hadn't known about wizands, but if they had found out they would not have been astonished. To them a wizand would have been something classifiable, a species of wood-demon, to be feared, perhaps, and if possible destroyed, but not incredible. To the people of Sophie's time a wizand was literally that—incredible. There was no place in their minds for such a concept.

So the wizand's first task in this new cycle was to discover as much as it could about those minds, and the only channel through which it could do this was Sophie. Hence her hunger to read. The wizand was not in fact troubled about her education as a witch. Her powers would come.

Time passed. The family moved south. When Sophie was thirteen her mother came into her room one evening and found her sitting cross-legged on the floor with her eyes shut and her old broomstick—the one Simon had made for her for that Halloween party at the Cotlands'—across her thighs, and her hands grasping either end. The pose looked otherworldly, hieratic, and in a curious way adult, or possibly ageless.

Sophie opened her eyes and smiled, perfectly friendly, but made a silent "Shh" with her lips. Her mother returned the smile and backed out.

"Sorry to shoo you out like that, Ma," Sophie said when she came downstairs. "I was just meditating. Belinda does it, and I thought I'd give it a go."

"With your old witch's broom?"

"The woman who explained it to Belinda says it's sometimes useful to hold onto something—something natural's best—Belinda uses a rock from the beach—and you sort of put your everyday stuff into that and tell it to stay there while the rest of you gets on with meditating. Anyway, my broomstick feels right. I knew it when it was a tree, remember."

"Maybe I should try it."

"If you can sit still for long enough. It's supposed to calm you down."

"You don't need it then. You're the calmest person I've ever met. I don't know where you get it from."

"I have to make up for you and Dad. Shall I lay the table?"

The bit about Belinda was true, except that Belinda had given up the experiment several months ago. Sophie had kept it in reserve as an explanation, if ever she needed it. And she wasn't surprised by what her mother had said about her calmness. Her friends had commented on it, and she was aware of it in herself. Nothing that happened to her, or might happen, moment by moment, was of any weight compared to her knowledge of what she was, or rather would be. She was like a seed, waiting to become a tree.

So, apart from giving in around the end of each October to what seemed to be a seasonal itch to fly, she made no practical use of the broomstick. Instead, every evening, she "meditated" with it across her lap. At first she merely passed on to the wizand all she had learnt during the day, not merely schoolwork and reading, but her interchanges with people, their sayings and doings. Later, when she had had her first period, she began to acquire her powers.

The wizand didn't exactly give them to her. They were there, and it showed them to her. It was as if it had shown her how to open a box of specialised instruments. They were, in fact, more like that than anything else she could think of. Though incorporeal, they seemed to her to have the shape and feel of old tools, used and reused by long-dead craftsmen, blades honed and rehoned, handles smoothed and made comfortable to grasp by the endless touch of confident, work-hardened fingers. They were also a kind of knowledge, like mathematical formulae such as builders have used since before the pyramids, but those are things that anyone can acquire. These were Sophie's, and Sophie's alone, just as they had belonged exclusively to each of the long line of the wizand's earlier symbiotes. That was why they were more like tools than formulae. Some of their shapes were very strange. It might be years before Sophie discovered what they were all for.

More time passed. When Sophie was fifteen she surprised her parents by telling them that she wanted to be a doctor. Simon was a designer, Joanne a history teacher, and they had assumed that when she went to University she would read English, or something like that. But she seemed both assured and determined, as she did about most things, in her quiet way, so they agreed to her taking the necessary A-levels. The wizand, of course, approved. Medical knowledge, though the knowledge itself had changed, was something within its experience. Sophie's reasons were similar. Healing was one of the things witches did. Medicine would provide a front. Witchcraft might help the healing process. So she worked hard, and got the results she needed in order to have some choice in the university she would go to, back in the north, where both she and the wizand belonged.

She took the broomstick with her and hung it on the wall of her room. Nobody thought this strange. Students keep all sorts of junk as totemic objects. Most days she meditated. This was equally normal. She made friends, easily, with anyone she liked the look of. It just happened, with no special effort on her part. More unnervingly—though it took a lot to unnerve her, these days—she found that she had only to look at some man with a feeling of mild physical interest on her part, and within a week or two he would have taken steps to get to know her, and be giving clear signals of wishing for something more, though she herself was merely borderline pretty, and that on her best days. She needed the presence of the man himself for this to work. It was no use going to a film and fantasising about Tom Cruise, but if he had happened to be visiting Leeds . . . No, once she'd discovered the effect, she'd have stayed clear. It wouldn't have been worth the risk.

After a while, very much in a spirit of sober experiment, she allowed some of these encounters to go further. The results could be physically satisfying, but not emotionally, because the men seemed unable to remain at her superficial level of involvement. Instead, whether she went to bed with them or not, they seemed to become not merely passionate but obsessed. She tried the obvious step of initiating the relationship via a carefully controlled fantasy, with definite rules of engagement, but it made no difference.

"Yes," said the wizand, when she told it.

"You mean that's just how it goes? It's no use trying to get them to understand I don't want them to feel like that about me."

"Say they don't," suggested the wizand.

"All right," said Sophie. "I'll give it a go."

She chose an archaeology student called Josh, already on the fringe of her circle, a healthy outdoor type with an affable personality. He had the advantage of being emotionally at a loose end, because his long-time girlfriend had decided to go and be a vet in New Zealand. He was standing at the bar in a pub talking rugby with his mates, with his back to Sophie, when she fantasised about spending a night with him in a tent in an owl-infested wood.

Ten minutes later he was sitting at her table. Within a week they were lovers.

She let his passion run for another ten days and then, one morning while they were dressing for his ritual run (she bicycled beside him for company), she took him by the hands and said, "Look me in the eyes, Josh."

He did so, frowning.

"Josh," she said slowly and quietly, "you don't love me anymore."

His frown deepened. He shook his head, naively bewildered.

"No," he said. "I suppose I don't. I'm sorry, Sophie."

"Don't worry," she said. "That's fine by me. We can go on as we are, if you want to. Just taking it easy on the emotional bit, if you see what I mean."

"All right," he said. "I suppose it was getting a bit unhealthy."

Sophie found the change a considerable improvement on her previous relationships, but it was still not fully satisfying. Josh made the point one evening, speaking thoughtfully out of a long silence.

"You've never been in love, have you, Sophie?"

"No, I suppose not. Not yet."

"I don't think you know how. You're just too cool. Not quite human."

She'd laughed, but inwardly accepted the point. Not quite human. Something else.

Despite that, the relationship worked for both of them, a steady companionship without emotional commitment. (Josh was planning to go out to New Zealand when his course ended, if his girlfriend didn't return before that.) So they were still together at the end of the academic year, and settled in as before at the start of the next term. Towards the end of October they took advantage of a late fine spell to go camping for a long weekend. Sophie chose the location, a valley merely glimpsed on a summer jaunt into the western hills, though the memory of that glimpse had kept sidling into her mind at irrelevant moments since. As she meditated the evening before they left the wizand said "Take me." It didn't occur to her not to do so.

They left the motorway and climbed a side road to a col, then began to descend a boulder-strewn hillside, bare apart from a large patch of old woodland a couple of hundred yards away on the left. Seen from this angle, Sophie recognised the place, recognised it from a single visit thirteen years before, a sulky child, slumped in the back of the car, barely glancing out of the window.

"Try along there?" she said.

"It doesn't look . . ."

He had already passed the turning. She was forced to use a little of her power, something she had avoided doing to him so far. She laid her fingers on his bare forearm.

"Please, Josh," she said.

He braked, reversed, and turned along the track. It was evidently not much used. The weeds along the centre rasped against the underside of the car. In places, anthills had encroached. Apart from the crawling car the hillside seemed entirely empty. Two sagging strands of rusty barbed wire blocked the entrance to the wood. Josh stopped and craned round to check for a turning place, but Sophie was already out of the car.

"For heaven's sake . . ." he called as she disentangled the loose post at one side of the entrance and dragged the wire clear, as she'd seen her father do thirteen years ago. She heard his call as if from much further away, but ignored it and walked on into the wood.

Fifty yards in, the track crossed a clearing, floored with the sort of fine, pale grass that grows in places mainly shadowed from the sun. To the right of it, at the edge of the trees, rose a low mound with a dip in the centre. There was a pile of cordwood stacked beside the track, ready for carting away.

Sophie stopped and looked around. Now there were two layers of recognition, both from thirteen years before, two visits, once by daylight with her father, once at midnight with the wizand. She hadn't connected them at the time, but now the memory of the second visit was far the stronger. She could hear, though far more faintly this time, the same high humming inside her head, and feel that nameless pressure all around her.

Josh came up behind her.

"What's up?" he said

He was so good natured that crossness didn't sound right in his voice—more as if he were putting it on because she was treating him badly and it was his duty to be cross about it.

"I'm sorry," she said. "I've just remembered. I came here once with my father. I went into a sort of daze, remembering. I suppose that's some sort of burial mound over there."

"Don't get them round here. It's probably a collapsed building. The high bit outside was the walls, and the dip's where the roof fell in. There's a deserted village down by the stream, if I'm thinking of the right place. Doctor Wedlow was going to lead a dig there, but something stopped it."

"Can we camp here?"

He sighed. It wasn't his idea of a camping place. He liked open, windy uplands.

"If you want to be eaten to death by mosquitoes," he said.

"There won't be any. I bet you."

"How much?"

"Dinner at Shastri's?"

"So I've got to be eaten before I can eat? Oh, all right. I'll get the car."

"Don't bring it all the way. Leave it on the track."

She didn't move. Dimly she heard the engine start, and stop. Josh's voice spoke behind her.

"What on earth did you put this in for?"

She didn't trouble to turn and look.

"It's due some fresh birch twigs. I'll use the old ones to light the fire."

Sophie pulled herself out of her half trance and helped set up the tent, and then to gather firewood. Josh liked to cook on these occasions, so she left him to fry sausages and chips and construct one of his pungent sauces while she cut twigs from a fallen birch beside the track. As she sat cross legged with the broomstick across her lap and shaped and bound the bundle into place, the yellow circular leaves fell from the twigs and scattered in a pattern around her, like iron filings round a magnet.

"Wake," said the wizand in her mind.

"How long?"

"Before midnight."

They opened a bottle of Rioja and ate by firelight, then sat companionably with a Jean Redpath tape playing, accompanied by owls, while they finished the wine. The high humming was louder now in Sophie's head, neither threatening nor benign, but with a meaning she couldn't interpret. She was aware, too, that she was using Josh for some purpose of the wizand's, and therefore of hers, but she didn't yet know what it was. Though she felt no guilt about this, she knew she must have no encumbrances, and therefore must repay all debts, so she troubled to attend to Josh and fit cheerfully into his mood, and when they went to bed to see to it that he was well satisfied. By now three owls were hooting from different parts of the wood and she could almost hear the mutter of a voice whispering some chant beneath the humming sound.

She knew at once when the time came, and turned Josh onto his back, leaned over him, pulled both eyelids down with her fingertip, whispered "Now sleep," and kissed him. Before she had withdrawn her lips he was asleep.

She wormed out of the sleeping bag and crawled naked from the tent. The broomstick leaned by the entrance. She took it to the mound, straddled it, leaned forward and whispered the word. The broomstick surged forward and up in a tight spiral to clear the trees. It was a full moon night, very bright, on the verge of frost. A few lights still glowed from the village a mile down the valley, and others speckled the darkness of the opposite slope. The broomstick headed directly downhill, flying only a few feet clear of the treetops.

Below the wood was a stretch of bare slope, and then small, stonewalled fields running along the bottom of the valley. Among them was an isolated copse, much smaller but even darker than the wood they had left. The broomstick headed directly for it, and as they came nearer Sophie saw that the trees were ancient yews, unlikely to be found growing wild in such a place, though there was no visible reason why anyone should have planted them there. A large modern prefabricated shed stood in the corner of the next field.

"There," said Sophie.

The broomstick swung aside, skimmed the roof of the shed, slowing all the time until she could alight as if from a still gently moving bicycle. At once it lost all buoyancy and became an apparently inert object. She laid it down and settled herself at the edge of the roof with her legs dangling into space, her elbow on her knee and her chin on her fist. The shed stood in its own patch of ground, rutted with wheel tracks and cluttered with bits of farm machinery, most of them engulfed in a tangle of brambles and nettles. The yew copse was immediately beyond the fence. The humming in Sophie's head had quieted as soon as they had left the clearing, to be replaced by a tenseness of expectation, a heavy stillness that spoke to her, saying "Wait." She was strongly aware of this being the appointed place and hour, but knew nothing of the event, and did not try to guess.

Time passed, enough for the moonshadows on the mat of ivy beneath the yews to have visibly shifted before the church clock in the village down the valley began to strike the midnight quarters. As the chimes floated past her the nape of Sophie's neck crawled, and her jaw muscles stiffened. She swallowed twice to ease them, then rose and moved back, crouching to peer over the rim of the roof. Her hand felt for the broomstick and gripped it.

In the pause that followed the quarters the ivy seemed to stir, as if a lot of small creatures were scurrying among it. As the first stroke of the hour reached the forgotten cemetery the tangled mat erupted and burst apart and the buried but never fully dead Community crawled into the air. The chill of the night changed its nature as the clean winter air mingled with the heavier cold of deep earth.

There was no reek of decay, because the flesh had not decayed, though the shrouds in which it had been buried had rotted centuries ago. But the bodies had held their shape, absorbing into themselves the weight and dullness of the clay in which they had lain, until they had become something like soft fossils.

Now they rose and moved into the open, grey in the moonlight, naked. They stared around. Who knows what they saw? The shadowy roofs and walls of the village where they had lived their human lives? Or the night as it now was, with only the old yews to mark their graveyard, and the strange-shaped modern barn beside it?

Sophie saw the grey faces begin to turn towards her and ducked down out of sight. Her throat was dry and her heart hammered. In her night flyings in other years she had felt the excitement of adventure, but never any fear, because she had always had the confidence that her powers, with the wizand's, were more than enough to keep her out of danger. But this time she understood she was in the presence of something whose power, whatever it consisted in, was at least equal to her own.

Carefully she raised her head and looked again. The Community were beginning to move now, all together, a grey mass shapeless as a cloud, crashing through the hedge into the lane, and on through the wall on the other side, tumbling the heavy stones out of their way, then on up the hill, following an ancient track untrodden for three hundred years. There was a gap in the next wall, blocked with barbed wire. The hooked points tore into their flesh as they strode through it, but no blood came. They crossed more fields and started up a bracken-shrouded slope.

The broomstick twitched in Sophie's hand. She straddled it, laid her body along it and spoke the word. The broomstick swept away and climbed the hill, well to the left of the line the Community was taking. They reached the wood together, and Sophie heard the crash of trampled undergrowth as the heavy remorseless limbs forced their way in under the trees. The broomstick skimmed the treetops, its new-cut birch twigs whistling sweetly wild as they sped through the still night air.

It slowed above the clearing and spiralled down, but before it reached the ground veered upward like a settling bird, allowing Sophie to reach out and grasp the side-branch of a sycamore bough that partly overhung the space below. Before the broomstick lost buoyancy she found a scrabbling foothold and managed to heave herself onto the main bough. She worked herself along it to a point where she would be clear for takeoff, laid her naked body against the flakey bark and drew the broomstick in beneath her right thigh.

The midnight moon shone down into the glade, lighting the tent where Josh lay asleep, and the logpile, and the mound that might once have been a dwelling. A silvery wisp of smoke still rose from the embers of the fire. The strange hum was back inside Sophie's head, quiet but persistent, with the chanting voice almost audible beneath it. No, more than one voice, several, chanting in unison, strong, quiet voices, certain of what they were doing, as Sophie was not yet certain.

The sounds of trampling drew nearer. Beneath her leg, Sophie felt the broomstick lose the tingle of secret life that was always there when she touched it.

"Hide," came the toneless voice in her mind.

Yes, she thought. I too have powers that these creatures might sense. She could indeed feel those powers wavering around her, like the tentacles of an anemone in a rock pool, so, just as an anemone does when its pool is disturbed, she retracted the charged network into herself and closed it away. A moment later the leaders of the Community crashed out into the open.

They paused. The grey faces stared at the glade, expressionless, but Sophie sensed a sudden check to the impulse that had drawn them here. They had come to do a particular thing, and found that thing no longer doable. Now they drifted across to the mound. Their groping arms patted the empty air, feeling for lost walls, a vanished door.

They turned and stared around again. For the first time they seemed to see the tent, and drifted towards it. Hands clutched the fabric and wrenched it away. Josh, locked in the sleep spell, didn't stir. They ringed him round, staring down.

Without word or signal certainty returned. Clay-chill hands seized Josh by the shoulders, dragged him from the sleeping bag and hauled him to his feet. He half woke and stared around, too bewildered for fear. His naked body was bone-white in the moonlight. While two of the creatures held him others turned to the woodpile. They carried the logs to the centre of the clearing and stacked them into a pyramid. Another crouched by the smouldering fire and blew on the embers. Others broke brushwood and piled it on, or stuffed it in among the logs. Smoke rose from the fire, silver white. A flame woke and flared, lighting the glade orange, but the grey bodies showed no tinge of it. Their stuff absorbed the light and sent none back.

When the logs were ready and the fire blazing they dragged Josh to the pile and used the tent cords to lash him spread-eagled against it. His mouth opened and closed in soundless shouts and pleadings. Sophie watched, tense, not with horror but with readiness. She had had no foreknowledge that this was going to happen. She had not brought Josh here to be a sacrifice, and would not have done so if she'd known, but she felt no guilt, only pity for his misfortune.

For herself, though, she felt excitement, eagerness, fulfilment. She was like the child of parents exiled from their country before she was born who has never herself been there, and now stands at last at a frontier station and gazes along a rail track receding through farmland, knowing that if she boards the approaching train it will take her to a life of struggle and danger, but also to the one place where she truly belongs, where she can be her whole self.

When the fire was well alight one of the creatures thrust a dry branch into it, waited for it to blaze up, and carried it flaming towards the pyre.

"Now," said Sophie in her mind.

In the broomstick the wizand woke. Sophie knelt, crouched, sprang. The broomstick swooped into the glade.

They made no sound, but at once grey faces turned. Grey arms rose in violent gestures, but struck too late as the broomstick whistled between them, levelled for an instant, and rose with Sophie grasping the flaming branch she had snatched as they swept past. Power poured down her arm and into the wood. Its lit end blazed into brilliance, trailing a path of flame behind it as they swung round the glade. Where it had been, the flame remained suspended.

Seven times they circled, building a wall of flame around the glade, prisoning the spellbound figures. When the seventh ring was steady in its place they rose and hovered above the centre. With her bare fingers Sophie broke fiery twigs from the branch and dropped them around the pyre. Where they fell, columns of fire remained, fencing Josh round. Then the broomstick rose higher and swept again round the glade, so that Sophie could reach out with the blazing branch to touch the trees and strip from them a storm of leaves, ash, sycamore, birch, beech, and oak, that spun whirling behind her, lit both by the flame she carried and the weaker fire below.

The humming sound was gone, and the voices were clear in her head, chanting in a language she had never before heard, but whose meaning she knew as if she had spoken it since she could talk. She knew the chanting voices too. They belonged to all the wizand's earlier symbiotes, of whom she was the latest. Their gathered power was the wizand's power, and now, while she lived, it was hers. As understanding came to her she joined the chant.

With the first word spoken the leaves fell. They rained down between the inner and the outer fire-rings, onto the reaching arms and the upturned faces and the ponderous bodies. Where they touched the grey flesh it lost its shape and crumbled away, as the bound souls that had held the people into their shapes found their release. Before the last leaf touched the woodland floor the clay-formed mob had vanished. All that was left of them was a layer of fresh earth spread in a ring around the pyre. At the same time the flames died away and the moon shone down on a naked man struggling with the cords that bound him to a pile of logs, until a naked woman walked out of the tree shadows behind him and whispered in his ear, and he slept.

The cords untied themselves at Sophie's touch. Effortlessly she lifted Josh free and carried him to where the tent had been. She unzipped the sleeping bag, settled him onto it, laid herself along his shuddering body, caressing the spasms into stillness. Then she whispered again in his ear.

"Wake up, Josh. You've been having a nightmare."

"Jesus! Haven't I just! Let me tell you about it!"

"Not now. In the morning. If you remember. Go back to sleep."

Obediently he slept. Sophie saw to it that he dreamed kindly dreams. Next, at her wish, the tent reformed itself around them, retying its cords, weaving its torn fabric into seamless sheets, sinking its pegs into the earth around. The log pile stacked itself as it had been, and grass recolonised the naked layer of earth. Housekeeping. The necessary cleanings and tidyings that have to follow any intrusion of supernatural energies into the natural world. In later years Sophie would deal with this kind of thing pretty well automatically, but now, being new to the task, she had to think about what she was doing.

Last of all, amused, she raised two small irritable bumps on her left arm and let Josh drift into wakefulness. She moved his hand to finger the place.

"You win your dinner," she whispered.

"Uh?"

"I got bitten."

"Told you so. Don't think I did. Great. Couldn't be better."

But for him it could. He woke fully and they made love again. This time, coolly, Sophie gave him not only herself, but selves of his own that he had never known were in him, strengths and delicacies, heightened senses and awareness, physical rapture too intense to last, but lasting and developing minute after minute until it died deliciously away. They lay together murmuring and caressing for a while, and then he fell asleep without any prompting from her.

Sophie turned on her back and gazed upward. Gently her fingertips stroked the two mosquito bites. If she'd chosen she could have wished them away, but she didn't. They were a different sort of housekeeping. Her powers hadn't been given her to win a bet, however tangential and silly. By the same token Josh must be fully paid, as she had just paid him, for what he had suffered. Simply taking the memory away would not have been enough. There would still have been a debt, though he wouldn't have known it. No debts. No obligations. No contracts, not with anything natural, anyone human. No loves.

Instead, power. Long ago, when she had asked the wizand whether it had anything to give her besides flight and leaf-sweeping, it had told her power, but not yet. When they had first flown, she had begun to understand its meaning, discovering the joy of flight, but also, more than that joy, the thrilling exhilaration of the power to fly. The same just now. Her body had greatly enjoyed their love-making—why not?—and she had taken pleasure in Josh's pleasure, but for her the main reward and fulfilment had been the use of her own power to give, or not to give.

And both of those things, the power to fly, the power to give, had been slight and momentary, trivial beside the thing she had discovered last night as she had swooped around the flame-ringed glade, chanting the language that is spoken both by angels and by demons, and the full weight and mass of her inheritance had poured into her, through her, out into the world, an ecstasy immeasurably beyond anything she had just given to Josh, as if she had laid her hand upon the web of forces that stays the material universe into its place, and felt that web vibrating to her touch.

She lost herself for a while, reliving the event. Slowly the memories faded and she returned to the here and now.

It was early dawn. The owls, silenced by the midnight riot, had not returned, but a couple of birds were whistling left over fragments of their full summer song. Sophie lay and thought about herself. No loves? At best, the sort of vague and already regretful affection she felt for Josh? No passions? No ecstasies? Things she could give to Josh, but not to herself? Yes, that was beyond her powers. She could have anything else, fame, wealth, love . . .

Love, without loving in return, is that love?

She sighed, and for a treacherous moment looked back. There had been a child once, difficult, wayward, passionate—what sort of life might she have had, but for the touch of an ash sapling?

If she had wished, Sophie could have summoned out of this very wood the stuff that had been Phyllida Blackett—ashes burnt over three hundred years ago, washed into this earth by winter rains, drawn by summer suns into branch and leaf, fallen and rotted into the earth again, cycle after cycle—summoned them and reformed them and caused Phyllida Blackett to walk once more across this glade, no wraith but the living flesh. It would have taken a tremendous exercise of power, but the power was there, hers.

So, surely, it would have been simple by comparison to call back the child Sophie had been, merely the spirit, for the flesh was already here, now, in this tent, and to let the child inhabit the flesh, imbue it with her old, passionate nature, so that she could love as well as be loved, love Josh, if for a season only, for these two days out only . . .

She wasn't conscious of having reached out and grasped the broomstick where she had laid it beside the sleeping bag, but she found she had done so, and now the wizand interrupted the reverie, speaking in her mind.

"No. I."

Automatically Sophie interpreted the two cryptic syllables, but the toneless voice in her head told her nothing of the wizand's own satisfaction at another phase in its life cycle safely embarked on in last night's orgasm of transferred powers.

*No, that is not for you. Never. I am your lover. I alone. I.*

## Phase A

Suppose Sophie had chosen, as she now had the power to, to look a generation or two into the future and see what would then have been happening in this glade where she lay, and in the valley beneath it, what might that future have been? If we assume no huge disrupting changes in the culture of the British Isles, and no accident to herself against which even her accumulated powers could not protect her, it would have been something like this:

In the glade itself, on the site of the present mound, stands a modest dwelling, made of modern materials but still very much in the spirit of the cottage in which Phyllida Blackett once lived, small-windowed, neat and unpretentious. Around it, growing surprisingly stoutly in so shaded a spot, is an orderly vegetable garden that includes a large plot of herbs, not all of them culinary.

A woman comes to the door. She is in late middle age, soberly dressed, well kempt and apparently healthy. Despite that there is a worn look about her, not tired, not tense or fretted, but with something of the air of a mediaeval statue on the west front of a great cathedral, purified by time and tempest, though in the woman's case the weather she has endured has been internal.

She has a broom in her hand with which she sweeps her doorstep. She replaces it behind the door and goes into the wood. There is no need to lock the door. Those brush strokes are ward enough.

Sophie's foreseeing eye doesn't follow her, but instead transfers its gaze to the village down the hill. Here not much has visibly changed. The public telephone box is a different shape and colour and is topped by a satellite dish. Most cars are electrical, and so on. But very few of the houses have been much altered, and despite the huge increase, nationwide, in the size of the average village, no new building has taken place here. It looks like a village where nothing much has happened for a long while.

Despite that, it has recently been in the news, thanks to a violent and public squabble between the vicar and his bishop, all the more surprising as the vicar has hitherto been one of those elderly ineffectual priests, drifting towards retirement, and meanwhile conducting soporific church services attended by only a handful of his older parishioners, out of habit. Why should such a man suddenly be granted a vision and a voice, the vision having more, apparently, to do with Satan than with God, but the voice so emphatic, so convinced and convincing, that parishioners who have attended the odd service out of curiosity to observe the change, have continued to come with steadily increasing fervour?

And when the bishop, hearing of this, has suggested to the vicar that some of the views expressed are verging on the heretical, have united behind him so unanimously that visiting journalists, looking for a jolly row between entrenched local worthies, have not been able to raise a single quotable slur?

These are early days still. It will be several years before the congregation definitively secedes from the mother church, and becomes more and more exclusive and reclusive as it unconsciously prepares itself to play its part, as necessary to the wizand as either of its two symbiotes, in what will perhaps be the final recurrence of that cyclical outburst of public witch frenzy that has so puzzled the historians of mediaeval Europe.

But it is not necessary to the wizand that Sophie should foresee any of that, and so she chooses not to.

# Talaria

VARRO ESCAPED INTO THE DESERT, as many, many slaves had done before him, whose bones now bleached among the dunes. Not his, though, or possibly not. It depended on the star maps.

Six weeks earlier, as part of the seven-yearly ritual cleansing of the household, he had been switched from his normal job in the stables and told to go and fetch and carry in the library, and there he had found the book. It was in Latin, a language few of these barbarians had bothered to learn—even Prince Fo's librarian had little more than a smattering. He hid it aside, and in snatched moments—the librarian evidently detested the cleansing and kept no discipline—he read it.

It purported to be a geography of Timbuktu and the region around it, compiled from travellers' accounts. Of course it was full of nonsense about Sphinxes and Sciopods and such, but here and there were patches of realism, details of trade routes and currency, descriptions of customs that Varro knew well from his five years in the city, and so on. The trade routes were no use to him. They were efficiently watched. The only hope was the desert. If you got a good enough start the bounty hunters wouldn't come up with you before they needed, for their own safety, to turn back. You could plod on, until the desert killed you.

To his astonishment and terror he found what he wanted, details of a forgotten route across the desert, far shorter than the still-used route around it, to one of Timbuktu's distant trading partners, Dassun. Most of the account was sensible, apart from the odd absurdity about a demon-guarded spring. There were neat little star maps. Varro studied the pages, his throat dry, his heart pumping, his palms chilly with sweat. He was a saddler by profession. Five years ago he had come to Timbuktu to explore the possibilities of trading his wares into the city, to the displeasure of the local guild, who had had him arrested on a false accusation of debt. Not only all his stock but his own person had been sold to pay the imaginary sum, the judge openly pocketing a third of it. As he had stood in the slave market he had vowed to Mercury, god of travellers, that if the opportunity to escape came he would take it. This was his first true chance.

Risking an hour, at least, beneath the lash he tore the two pages from the book, added a map of the city and its surroundings, folded them and tucked them into his loincloth. He was reasonably sure he wouldn't be searched on leaving the library. His master maintained it only because a nobleman should have such a thing, so as far as the rest of the household were concerned there was nothing worth stealing in it.

The slaves slept on the roof of their quarters. Studying the stars, and thus checking the accuracy of the maps, was no problem. Slaves played knucklebones in their spare time, wagering trivial items they'd been able to filch during the day. Varro understood the odds better than most, but took care to let the others think he was just a lucky player. As a saddler he already had a good knife, and now began, grudgingly, to accept scraps of food in part settlement of bets. He couldn't hoard openly for the journey, because of the certainty of betrayal. Every other slave would be whipped when he was found to have gone, on the assumption that at least one of them must have helped him, whereas any of them who prevented an escape would be given a tiny share of the notional bounty. Some of the slaves were expert in such betrayals. One, in particular, a man called Karan, had roused unfounded suspicions that had cost Varro the lives of two of his friends.

Slaves were issued annually with a length of cotton from which to make their own clothes. Varro, typically, had some to spare, and it was natural enough for him to use it to refurbish the shoulder bag in which he kept his belongings, casually enlarging it as he did so. There was not much more that he could do.

He was worried about his feet. Slaves went barefoot, so his soles had thickened, but five years in a household, years spent mainly at a saddler's bench, are no preparation for days of desert marching. Of course it would have been easy for him to make his own sandals, with all the materials to hand at his workbench, but on his first day at work the harness master had told him about a predecessor who had been found doing exactly that, and what had been done to the man before he died. Varro had thought it an exaggeration. Then, not now. His friends had died not only to satisfy Prince Fo's notion of justice but also his taste in entertainment. It wasn't even worth the risk of filching leather. All he dared take from work on his last day at the bench was a few small tools, needles and fine cord. That and his supply of food and an empty waterskin were already dangerous enough.

There was a rota of the younger men told off to attend the slave-master in his room each night, but the man wasn't picky—almost anyone with flesh on his arse would do. In fact, the offer to take over this chore was one of the regular items gambled at knucklebones, which was how Varro had managed to avoid it so far. On his chosen night he made the offer and then deliberately lost his bet, so nightfall found him scratching at the slave-master's door.

"Hum, Varro? Thought it was Gabrin coming. Dice fall badly for you this time?"

Varro hung his head as if in shame.

"No, sir. Gabrin has the runs," he muttered.

“Greedy sod, if it’s true. Let’s take a look at you, man. Hold your head up. I’m not going to hurt you.”

As an apprentice Varro had learnt to use a knife for other things than trimming leather. He let the slave-master chuck him under the chin and drove his knife in beneath the raised arm. The slave-master choked and collapsed to the floor. Now there was no turning back.

In addition to the all-round lashings for his escape, there would now be at least one death, after torture. Varro wiped his finger along the blade and used the blood to scrawl the name “Karan” on the floor by the slave-master’s outstretched hand, then smeared more blood onto the man’s forefinger. He took the keys from the man’s belt, and explored the room for anything he could use. The shoes were all too small, but the open-toed sandals, though ornate and shoddy, were better than nothing. He took three pairs, a cloak to cover his slave garments, and a purse of coins. No doubt there was more hidden in the room, but he hadn’t time to search. Finally he filled his waterskin at the pitcher and drank as much as he could stomach. The room was at the entrance to the slave quarters, so he could let himself straight out.

From the roof he had studied the movements of the household watch—his fellow slaves, but no less a danger for that. He moved through shadows, avoiding them, to the back of the stables, where the bedding was still being cleared out into the dung-carts, nocturnal work because in the cooler air the odours would be less offensive to his lordship’s nostrils. At a point when all the barrows were indoors being loaded he gathered a bundle of loose straw under his arm, and waited, and when the work seemed almost done took a similar chance to climb up, tuck himself down between the main heap and the side panel of the cart, and spread the straw over himself. The last few barrowloads were pitchforked aboard, adding to his concealment. The oxen started to heave the cart away on the slow journey to one of his Lordship’s estates.

These lay northeasterly of the city, so as soon as the cart was well clear of the gates Varro wriggled to the back, slipped over the tailboard, dropped, and darted to the side of the road. He lay there, panting, until the wheels were out of earshot, then rose and headed south, steering by the stars. Prince Fo was endlessly fussing with his harness, and often took a saddler with him on his hunting trips along the edge of the desert, if only to have someone to beat when his saddle chafed, so Varro had a good idea of where he was.

Daybreak found him well into the desert, where no sane man travels much after sunrise, but he trudged on for as long as he could bear to, and then found a rock on a north-facing slope with a thin strip of shade from which he could watch back the way he had come. By now the slave-master's sandals were falling apart. It was difficult to sleep for anxiety, heat, thirst and discomfort, so he spent part of the day taking the ruined sandals apart and using the pieces to adjust and reinforce the next pair.

He walked all that night, hurrying, because even with the stars to guide him and the memorised list of landmarks from the manual, he knew he might finish the stage only in the rough vicinity of the water hole, and then would need daylight to find it. As dawn broke he came to three separate sets of animal tracks converging in the same direction. He walked on until he came to harder ground and turned aside in the direction that the animal prints had taken, along a line that should intersect with them. Ten minutes later he was kneeling by a scummy pool in a hollow.

First he poured a libation to Mercury, then drank sparingly and filled his waterskin. He drank again, twice, before heading off, still aside from his route and still on hard ground, and didn't start searching for shade until he was well clear of the pool.

This time he slept well. In the late afternoon he woke and returned to the pool, where he tied a large loop with a slipknot into his toughest cord, laid it out along the water's edge, and led the loose end up to the rim of the hollow, and hid. In the evening small animals came to the pool to drink, but they were very quick and wary, and seemed able to smell where he had been. They sniffed around the noose and went elsewhere.

He had two long nights' journey to the next water, so couldn't afford to watch too long. In the late dusk he filled his skin with what he could carry, and his stomach also, and set out. By next morning his sandals were again in ruins, so he spent some of the day cobbling a last pair together, and set out again in the dusk. His food was by now almost gone, so while he trudged on he tried to devise more effective animal traps in his mind.

This place, he hoped, would be easier to find. There was a sort of notch in a range of hills, the outlines clearly described. His way led through the notch, on the left flank of which water oozed down a rock. It turned out to be exactly so. He praised Mercury, and poured a second libation for the soul of the long-dead traveller who had written the manual. The water was sweet and clean, but the only sign that any animals came there was a scattering of bird droppings. He saw no nests and heard no cries. Nevertheless he tried laying out nooses for them, but none came all day.

He moved on that evening, knowing that if he didn't find food at the next water place, or sooner—it was another two nights' journey—he wasn't going to make it through the desert. It amused his sardonic turn of mind to think that this was the supposedly demon-guarded pool. It had been made by men, ages before, and had what was apparently a small temple beside it. The demon might be the statue of some forgotten god. Perhaps the priests who had served it had demanded a human sacrifice, which would help to explain the sudden little absurdity in the otherwise reasonable and accurate route details. Well, if it didn't provide him with something to eat, he thought, the demon would get its payment of a life.

He reached the water on the verge of delirium. By the second midnight his shoes had fallen apart. His feet were already blistered, and now slowed him to a hobble. He was weak for lack of food.

If the last section of his route hadn't lain along a valley, delaying the apparent sunrise, he would never have made it. Even so, by the time he found the place the landscape was wavering before his eyes, what had begun as a plea to Mercury would end up in fragments of nursery rhyme, and the pitiless sun had become one enduring blow against his flank and shoulder, to send him reeling, then lie among the rocks, and die.

The valley floor dipped suddenly. He stood at the rim of a shallow slope and gazed down. There was the pool, a stone-rimmed circle with steps leading to the water. Beside it, exactly as described, stood a little roofless temple, a flagged paving from which rose a dozen squat, barbaric pillars. No demon, of course, but, confirming his conjecture, the headless image of some large winged quadruped—ludicrous anatomy—that had fallen opposite the steps, lay between the temple and the pool.

Cautious as ever, despite his desperate need, he crawled down the slope rather than risk a fall, and on down the steps to drink. The lowest steps were in the shade, so having drunk as much as was safe, and poured his libation, he turned and sat with his bleeding feet in the water. From down here he could see nothing but the excellent masonry of the wall, vast blocks fitted so well that there was nowhere he could have driven a knife between them. Above that the unornamented rim of the pool. Above that the intense harsh blueness of the sky. And, between the rim and the sky, a single large eye, watching him.

A single eye, because the thing was watching him sideways, bird-fashion, though the eye was much too large for that of any bird—indeed of any creature that he knew. He could now see the beginnings of the curve of an immense, hooked beak, and a fringe of small feathers, though the scalp seemed bald. Surely, even half-delirious, he would have noticed that head on the fallen statue. No, the thing had seemed headless, but clearly a mammal, with the only plumage on the wing, the rest of the body the same colour as the sandstone desert rocks, from which he had assumed it to be carved. The head must have been tucked away out of sight, bird-fashion again.

He was startled, but not for the moment terrified, in fact not much more than wary. When the creature rose and came for him, then would be the time for terror. But the only move it made was to lay its head back down somewhere out of sight. The movement didn't look like that of a hunter, withdrawing for a stealthy approach, more like that of an exhausted animal, momentarily interested in the arrival of another creature, but then deciding that the intruder was no threat and returning to its rest.

Varro drank again and half filled his skin, just in case, then rose and climbed the steps, watching over his shoulder as the creature came into view. It was indeed huge, not as big as an elephant, but half again the size of any ox he had ever seen. Apart from the scalp, the neck was feathered as far as the shoulders, and the body beyond that furred, both a rusty yellow-brown, the colour of the desert. A vast wing, desert coloured too but barred light and dark, lay along its flank.

It seemed to have lost interest in him and made no move as on wincing feet he crept round the pool and climbed the temple steps and turned. Seeing it from above he recognised at once what the thing was. The dark tuft at the end of the almost naked tail was the giveaway. A gryphon. The body of a lion and the head and wings of an eagle. Ridiculous. Anatomically impossible. There, in front of him.

Delirium? How does a man prove to himself that he isn't mad, when the very proof may be merely part of the madness? His feet, so much more conscious of their soreness now that they had been cosseted a little? In a futile attempt to validate the proof Varro sat down on the steps and inspected them. Something had carved a half-inch gash into the ball of his left foot. Further back, what had begun as a blister was now raw flesh. There was a matching, but larger, sore on his right foot, as well as a dozen minor cracks and abrasions either side. Well bandaged, and with good shoes, they might be fit to walk on in a week. Academic. He would be dead of starvation well before that.

The gryphon sighed. He looked up and saw the vast flanks still collapsing from the breath. Otherwise the creature hadn't stirred. He returned to his feet.

He was painfully picking grit out of one of the cracks with the butt of a needle when the gryphon sighed again. This time Varro listened, and heard in the indrawn breath before the sigh, a low, half-liquid rattling sound, that made the import of the sigh itself instantly clear. The monster was sick.

Dying?

He rose and hobbled round to where he could see the thing sideways on. The head lifted and for a moment the round eye—darker than gold, the colour of sunset—gazed at him. There was death in that eye. The head fell back, indifferent.

Death. "The demon of the well demands a death." This time it would have two, its own, and Varro's.

A delirium notion wandered into his mind. *But it only needs one. Why mine?* He giggled, and pulled himself together. There was meat on that carcass, but he couldn't wait for it to die. He must kill it. How?

As Varro studied the huge animal in this fresh light it sighed again, and this time slowly stretched a foreleg. The claws were already extended, but they seemed to stretch further with the movement. Each was as long as Varro's middle finger, but twice as thick at the base and curving to a savage point. Even a dying blow from such a weapon would be lethal. He would need to come at the creature from behind its back.

It was lying on its left side, so the heart was presumably out of reach. Slit its throat? The dense plumage of the neck prevented a quick, clean strike. But once, on a crossing of the Alps, Varro had watched the train captain deal with a pony that caught its leg in a cranny and broke it. The pony's load had been precious and fragile. The pony, trapped half upright, but threshing around in agony, would in another couple of seconds have dragged itself free and fallen, but the train master had darted in, gripped the load with his left hand, and with his right driven a blade no longer than Varro's hilt-deep into the soft strip between the collarbone and the neck, then taken the weight of the load while a pulsing jet of blood arched clean across the track. With decreasing struggles the pony had collapsed, and before long died.

Varro returned to the temple and honed his knife point on one of the steps. Though the appearance of intelligence in animals can be very deceptive, especially in birds (how bright, really, is a lark?), there was something about the creature's patient dying that made Varro feel that it might understand what he was up to, and why. But the only move it made as he went round and crouched behind the shoulders was to raise its head and watch him again. He reached out, testing, tensed to snatch himself away if the fierce beak darted to attack, but the creature continued to watch him steadily as he shifted to choose the spot at which to strike. The train master had clearly known the exact run of a large artery in the pony's neck. Varro had almost two handspans to choose from, and could only guess.

As his hand poised for the blow the monster laid its head back on the paving and stretched its neck a little, much as a brave man might, making things easier for the surgeon.

"Mercury, God," Varro whispered, "guide this hand."

Summoning his last strength, he plunged the knife in at a slight angle, forced the hilt forward to widen the inward cut, then flung himself back as the monster's body convulsed, once. He rose and stood, gasping. Instead of a jet, a pulsing gush of blood was welling from the wound, so rapidly that by the time Varro looked it had begun to spread across the paving, draining towards the pool. The colour seemed no different from that of his own blood, or any other animal he knew of. He went and sat on the steps, watching the life fade out of that sunset eye.

He found he was shuddering, partly from exhaustion and the aftershock of violent and dangerous action, but also from the knowledge (though not the understanding) of what he had done. Though both had seemed necessities, this was something wholly different from the killing of Prince Fo's slavemaster. The world had been well rid of such a man. The gryphon . . . there was no code by which he could value the gryphon's life against his own. Good or ill, he knew he had done something portentous. What would the gods feel? Mercury had many responsibilities, being god, along with travellers, of science, commerce and healing, tricksters, vagabonds and thieves, and all merry fellows. He seemed to have answered Varro's prayer and guided his blade point to the artery, which in turn seemed to suggest that he had no particular fondness for gryphons, but how could Varro know which of the captious deities might feel otherwise?

He went down to the pool again and poured a libation to the unknown god before he drank. Already the water tasted of blood. There was no point yet in washing. He had gorier work to do, but he needed to rest, so waited until as much of the blood as was going to had drained from the carcass. Even then he took the precaution of stripping naked before he started his butchery.

Skinning a gryphon proved little different from skinning a horse or bullock—all part of his apprenticeship. He did it systematically, as if sparing the leather that no one would ever have a use for. When he had loosed a flap large enough to fold back he cut out the huge right lung and exposed the heart. He cut that out and folded the flap of hide back over the flesh. Exhausted again by now he carried the heart up into the shade of one of the temple pillars, where he sliced small pieces off it and chewed them slowly, feeling the strength flow back through his body. By the time he had eaten enough the sun was almost overhead and the first vultures had arrived.

He dragged the loose lung a little way up the slope to distract them and then drove them away from the main carcass with rocks. Splashing himself often with water from his skin he toiled on, first constructing a meat cache out of fallen masonry, storing the liver in it, and then cutting out the rest of the innards and hauling them off for the birds. Next he cut and cached as much meat as he could eat in a fortnight, pulled the hide back over what remained and weighted it with boulders, and at last went and bathed in the now reeking pool. The sun had dried him by the time he returned to the temple.

Staggering and hazed with tiredness he tied cords between three pillars, draped his stolen cloak across them and lay down in its triangle of shade. The harsh cries of the vultures threaded through his dreams, which were of the gryphon still alive, but with half its hide stripped from its flank. As it snarled and slashed at a ring of prancing scavengers an outer ring of monsters—centaur, sphinx, basilisk, hydra, gorgon—watched lamenting. Mercury presided dry-eyed with a god's half smile.

It was dusk when Varro woke. The gryphon's hide had proved too tough for the vultures, but they had pecked out the great sunset eye.

There was a good moon, so he continued to dismember the gryphon far into the night, dragging most of the meat away for the vultures, and again next morning until the heat became intolerable. He rested out the worst of it and worked methodically on, careful not to break his knife, impatient with a joint. By late afternoon he had removed enough of the meat and bones to be able to heave the remains of the carcass over, and by nightfall he had the hide free, and almost whole, apart from the two large holes he had cut in order to be able to drag it over the wings. This had been his main aim. With it he could create a bigger and denser area of shade than was possible with the cloak and cloth. He dragged it up to the temple and laid it out, pelt upward, between the pillars. It was larger than he needed. There would be enough left over for him to add a hammock to his plans. He continued to work by moonlight, trimming rawhide thongs from its edges, until he was exhausted, at which point he folded the pelt in on itself several times and slept on it in more comfort than he had done since they had taken him to the slave-market. He did not dream at all.

By the third noon he had both awning and hammock in place, and strips of gryphon flesh drying in the sun, protected from the vultures by a structure of rib bones. That evening he started making his new shoes.

Here he had had two strokes of what seemed again to be god-given good fortune. While wrestling the hide loose he had planted a foot beside one of the wing roots for purchase as he heaved, and had noticed how neatly at that point the pelt that covered the sinews around the wing root matched the shape of his foot, running a handsbreadth up the wing bone beside his ankle. He was looking at the upper of a shoe, ready-made on the animal. Carefully he now cut loose the whole patch of pelt that he had left around the wing root, slitting it down the back of the heel to get it free of the wing. Then the same on the other side.

The soles he had also found already half-made. The beast's immense pads, though almost circular, were each longer than his own foot, the skin as thick as the width of his thumb. He soaked his chosen pieces in the pool, then laid them out in the sun, urinated on them, folded them hair-side inward, covered them with sun-warmed rocks and left them to begin to putrefy. He then slept out the rest of the day.

When he woke he started to fashion crude tools from the beast's bones and the rocks of the desert, and also hammered some of the long bones and extracted the marrow, which he mixed with part of the gryphon's brain. By now he judged that the pieces he had set aside would have decayed enough for the hairs to begin to loosen in the follicles, so he laid them out on a cylinder from a fallen pillar and with the roughened inner side of one of the ribs rubbed the hair free. That done he turned them over and used his knife, sharpening it again and again, to slice away the innermost layer of the skin, exposing the true leather, which he set to soak in the pool while he ate. Lastly by moonlight he hollowed a shallow bowl in the earth, lined it with a single piece of hide, and used it to compound a reeking mix of water, marrow and brain. He then slept, again without dreams.

When he woke he drew his pieces of hide out of the pool and laid them out in the rising sun, while he cut more strips of the meat to dry beside them. Another day, his nose told him, and what was left would be no longer safe to eat. He worked on his tools for a while, turning the pieces of hide over from time to time until they were no more than moist. Now he smeared his mixture onto them, and worked it in until they were again saturated, and then laid them out to dry once more. When they were again merely moist he spread them onto the fallen pillar and rubbed and stretched and rolled and pounded them steadily for several hours. By the time night fell he had four cuts of true leather, crude but both supple and strong, even now that the water had dried right out of it. It was far better than he could possibly have hoped for. One might well have thought it had spent weeks, if not months, in the tanner's vats.

Next morning, the eighth of his stay at the gryphon's pool, he cut the pieces to shape and stitched them together, hissing peacefully at his work as he had always used to at his own bench in Ravenna. It was a long while since he had felt anything like this contentment. Before he tried the shoes on he inspected his feet, and was surprised to find how well they had mended while he had been busy with other matters. For this he dutifully praised Mercury, god, among everything else, of healing.

What he had made turned out to be short boots, rather than shoes, running neatly up just beyond the ankle bones and lacing down the back. What is more, they were amazingly comfortable, a pleasure to wear. In them he was able to walk far more easily than he would have dreamed possible a few days back.

All the bits of carcass he had strewn around the place were now picked bare. Apart from what was in Varro's cache nothing remained except bones, a feathered skull with an amazing beak, and the hide slung between the temple pillars. As the sun went down on his ninth day he took that down, folded it and piled masonry over it. One day, perhaps, he would be able to come back for it. He might even make a saddle out of it, if the leather wasn't ruined by then.

Five days later, still feeling reasonably strong, Varro reached a nomadic encampment at the far edge of the desert. The herders spoke no language that he knew, and would take no payment for their hospitality, but when he spoke of Dassun in a questioning tone they set him on his way with gestures and smiles. Later there was farmed land, with villages, and a couple of towns, where he paid for his needs from the slave master's purse, and finally, twenty-seven days after his escape, he came to Dassun.

The city was walled but the gates unguarded. Inside it seemed planless, tiny thronged streets, with gaudy clothes and parasols, all the reeks and sounds of commerce and humanity: houses a mixture of brick, timber, plaster, mud and whatnot, often several storeys high; the people's faces almost black, lively and expressive; vigorous hand-gestures aiding speech; the fullness of life, the sort of life that Varro relished.

He let his feet tell him where to go and found himself in an open marketplace, noisier even than the streets—craftsmen's booths, merchants' stalls of all kinds grouped by what they sold, fruit, fish, meat, grain, gourds, pottery, baskets and so on. Deliberately now, he sought out the leatherworkers' section.

He approached two stall-holders, both women, and showed them his tools, and with obvious gestures made it clear that he was looking for work. Smiling, they waved him away. The third he tried was an odd-looking little man, a dwarf, almost, fat and hideous, but smiling like everyone else. He would have fetched a good price as a curiosity in any northern slave market. He chose a plain purse from his stall, picked a piece of leather from a pile, gave them to Varro and pointed to an empty patch of shade beneath his awning. Varro settled down to copy the purse, an extremely simple task, so for his own pleasure as well as to show what he could do he put an ornamental pattern into the stitching. When the stall-holder came back to see how he was getting on, Varro showed him the almost finished purse. The stall-holder laughed aloud and clapped him on the shoulder. He pointed at his chest.

"Andada," he said.

"Andada," Varro repeated, and then tapped his chest in turn and said "Varro."

"Warro," the man shouted through his own laughter, and clapped Varro on the shoulder again. Varro was hired.

That night Andada took him home and made him eat with his enormous family—several wives and uncountable children, each blacker than the last, and gave him a palliasse and blanket for his bed. The children seemed to find their visitor most amusing. Varro didn't mind.

Over the next few days, sitting in his corner under the awning and copying whatever Andada asked him to, Varro shaped and stitched out of scraps of leather a miniature saddle and harness, highly ornate, the sort of thing apprentices were asked to do as a test-piece before acceptance into the Guild.

Andada, when he showed it to him, stopped smiling. He took the little objects and turned them to and fro, studying every stitch, then looked at Varro with a query in his eyes and made an expansive gesture with his hands. Varro by now had learnt some words of the language.

"I make big," he confirmed, and sketched a full-size saddle in midair.

Andada nodded, still deeply serious, closed his stall, and gestured to Varro to follow him. He led the way out of the market, through a tangle of streets, into one with booths down either side. These clearly dealt in far more expensive goods than those sold in the market, imported carpets, gold jewellery set with precious gems, elaborate glassware, and so on. Halfway up it was a saddler's shop, again filled with imports, many the standard Timbuktu product, manufactured for trade and so gaudy but inwardly shoddy—a saddler who produced such a thing for Prince Fo would have been flogged insensible.

Andada gripped Varro's elbow to prevent him moving nearer.

"You make?" he whispered. Varro nodded, and they went back to the market. He spent an hour drawing sketches of different possible styles. Andada chose three, then took Varro to buy the materials, casually, from different warehouses, among other stuff he needed for his normal trade. Varro watched with interest. From his experience with the guild in Timbuktu he saw quite well what was happening. There was good money in imported saddles. Andada by making them on the spot could undercut the importers with a better product. The importers would not like it at all.

Andada was a just man, as well as being a cautious one. Having done a deal that allowed one of the importers to conceal the provenance of Varro's saddles, and leave a handsome profit for both men, he started to pay Varro piecework rather than a wage, at a very fair rate, allowing Varro to rent a room of his own, eat and drink well, and for the moment evade the growing prospect of finding himself married to one or more of Andada's older daughters. He started to enjoy himself. He liked this city, its cooking, its tavern life, its whole ethos, exotic but just as civilised as Ravenna, in its own way. So as not to stand out he adopted the local dress, parasol, a little pill box hat, thigh-length linen overshirt, baggy trousers gathered at the ankle . . .

But not the slippers. While his fellow citizens slopped in loose-heeled flip-flops, he stuck to the gryphon-hide boots he had made for himself in the desert. They were the only footwear he now found comfortable, so much so that on waking he sometimes found that he had forgotten to take them off and slept in them all night. Presumably, in the course of that last hideous stretch to the gryphon's pool, he had done some kind of harm to his feet, from which they had only partially recovered—indeed, unshod, they were still extremely tender—but had managed to adapt themselves to the gryphon boots during the long march out of the desert. It was almost two months before he discovered that there was more to it than that.

Unnoticed at first, he had begun to feel a faint tickling sensation on the outside of both legs, just below the top of the shoes at the back of the ankle bone. He became conscious of it only when he realised that he had developed a habit of reaching down and fingering the two places whenever he paused from his work. The sensation ceased as soon as he unlaced the boots and felt beneath, but though he could find nothing to cause it on the inside of the boots themselves, it returned as soon as he refastened them. It was not, however, unpleasant—the reverse, if anything—so he let it be and soon ceased to notice it.

So much so that it must have been several days before he realised that the sensation was gone. He explored, and found that where it had been there was now a small but definite swelling in the surface of the boots, but nothing to show for it when he felt beneath, apart, perhaps, from a slightly greater tenderness of his own skin at those two places. The swellings had grown to bumps before the first downy feathers fledged.

He studied them, twisting this way and that to see them, and then sat staring at nothing.

*Talaria,* he thought. *The winged boots of the God Mercury. Impossible. But nothing is impossible to a god. Talaria. Mine.*

Varro's attitude to the gods had always been one of reasoned belief. He didn't think, suppose he had been ushered into the unmitigated presence of a deity, and unlike Semele could endure that presence, that he would have seen a human form, or heard a voice speaking to him through his ears. Whatever he might have seen and heard he would done so inside his head. The human shape and speech were only a way for him to be able to envisage the deity and think about him. Similarly with the talaria. Suppose Mercury had chosen to appear to him in human form, he would have done so with all his powers and attributes expressed in his appearance, including that of moving instantaneously from one place to another. The talaria were, so to speak, a divine metaphor. Now the god was presenting him with a real pair. To what end? So that when the wings had grown he could fly instantaneously back to Ravenna? He wasn't sure that he wanted to. He liked it here.

Another few days and the little wings were clearly visible, bony, pale and pitiful beneath the scant down. They would have been a distinct embarrassment with Roman dress, but the trousers he was now wearing fastened just below them and there was plenty of room for them in the loose-fitting legs. Indeed, he himself barely noticed them during the day, and spent his time as usual, but at night when he took the boots off and laid them beside his bed the wings started to beat in pitiful frenzy. They quieted at his touch, but fell into their frenzy again as soon as he let go, so in the end he took them into his bed and let them nestle against his chest, where they were still.

They were, he realised, in some sense alive. Faint quiverings ran through them in their sleep. He found their companionship comforting, taking him back to a time early in his apprenticeship when he had found a stray puppy and adopted it for his own until it had grown big enough to become a nuisance about the household and his master's wife had insisted on its banishment. He hadn't minded that much. Growing, the animal had lost its charm, but he could still remember the pleasure he had taken in it when it had been smaller. He felt something of the same protective affection for the talaria.

It took a while for the first true feathers to fledge, and by then the boots were changing in other ways. Their tops were creeping up his calves, bringing the wings with them, and also the stitching down the lower part of the heel. There were still the same five lace-holes on either side of each boot, and the same dozen crisscross stitches, but below that the leather had simply joined itself up, with a faint seam marked mainly by the flow of the hairs. All this made the boots increasingly tiresome to remove. So if he was tired, or a little drunk after a pleasant evening in a tavern, he tended to sleep in them.

Looking back later he sometimes wondered how long he had been concealing from himself what was really happening to him. The truth was thrust in his face one evening at the start of the hot weather—apparently they were due a month of appalling temperatures before the blissful onset of the rains—and Andada took him down, along with all the family, to bathe in the immense river that ran a mile from the city walls. Almost the whole city seemed to be there, each section of the community bathing in its designated place. They all stripped off, men, women, and children, and waded in together, with a great deal of shouting and splashing and general horseplay to keep the crocodiles away—or so they claimed, though Varro guessed that the natural high spirits of these people would make them behave like that if nothing more aggressive than a newt inhabited the river. Afterwards the children rushed screaming up and down the shore while the adults lay chatting on the sandy earth, the more fastidious with a scrap of cloth over their privacies. Varro was popular. He had an excellent stock of tall stories picked up from the adventures of his fellow slaves, and a dry way of telling them which these people found amusingly different from their own ebullient style. (He kept quiet, of course, about his own slavery, and also about gryphons.)

He was chatting with a neighbour when one of Andada's younger offspring scampered up, stopped, stared for a moment, pointed, and exclaimed, "Funny feet, Warro got!"

Several adults snapped at the child. Remarks about a person's appearance were considered extremely offensive. The child's mother snatched him away, apologising over her shoulder as she led him off. The nature of the whole exchange made Varro realise that everyone around had been aware of the peculiarity, but by then he had recovered his poise enough to shrug and say, "Forget it. It's true, anyway. It's not a disease, just a deformity that runs in my family. That's why I wear these boots. I'll put them on so you don't have to look at my feet."

To conceal the wings he had with some difficulty removed boots and trousers as if they had been a single garment. His companions looked elsewhere as he put them on the same way, but far more easily. As the light died they built fires of driftwood all along the shore and roasted gobbets of meat and sweet roots and passed them round. But the sense of embarrassment, of something not entirely acceptable about Varro, hadn't fully faded by the time they were walking home from the river under the stars. Varro carried one of the sleeping children slung over his shoulder and Andada walked beside him with another, gossiping all the way, obviously aware of his need for support.

Another man in Varro's position would have gone out and got very drunk. Varro preferred to keep his liquor for pleasure, so he merely went back to his room, lit his lamp, removed his boots and studied his feet with care. Again, this must have been something that he had subconsciously avoided doing for a long while.

He had known, of course, that the skin was tender, but hadn't realised how thin it had become all over the foot, including the sole. No wonder he had found the few barefoot paces down into the water and back up the shore that evening so uncomfortable. The nails were soft and tender too, and more pointed than rounded, but not very noticeably so, any more than the unusual breadth and stubbiness of the feet themselves seemed actually freakish. The thing that must have caught the child's attention was the position of the big toes, each of which had separated itself from the other four by moving backward over an inch, so that it now lay alongside the ball of the foot.

As Varro put the boots on again the wings—fully fledged now, desert-coloured, barred dark and light—gave a little flutter of pleasure, like a dog cavorting on being taken for an unexpected walk.

By now the gates of the city were closed, so Varro climbed up onto the unguarded walls and walked round to the northern side of the city. Here he leaned on the parapet and gazed out towards the desert.

It was quite clear to him what was happening. It wasn't only the boots that had brought it about. *I have eaten the gryphon's heart, eaten its flesh,* he thought. *I have slept on its hide, I have bathed in its blood. I could abandon the boots, but still it would happen.*

He remembered the magnificent strange creature that he had killed. He remembered the life fading out of that sunset eye.

Next day he asked Andada to close the stall early and took him up to his room. In the stifling dim heat he told him his whole story, rolled up his trousers and showed him the boots. Tentatively Andada reached to touch a wing, but it shrank from his hand.

"Warro, what is happening to you?" he whispered. "Witchcraft?"

"Godcraft, more like," said Varro. "Mercury enjoys a joke."

"I know a clever woman. Expensive, but I pay."

"You are a good man, Andada, a good friend. I haven't had a friend like you for a long while. But when a god decides, there is nothing anyone can do. Everything I might try would serve, one way or another, to make it happen. But it is not so bad as you might think. I shall be free—freer than most men. And you will be rich. And unless my whole nature changes we will still be friends. Listen. This is what I want you to do . . ."

Varro stayed in the city, enjoying its life and constructing saddles to any pattern he fancied, until his toenails began to grow through the toes of his boots, each point as sharp and hard as a steel bradawl. He could have carved rock with them. His feet were now unmistakably paws, and he was walking with a strange, catlike lope. He was already wearing a long, loose cloak all day, for though his wings had migrated to the small of his back their tips trailed almost to the ground, and his tufted tail was not much shorter.

He said good-bye to Andada's wives and children, giving each of them a handsome present, and headed north with Andada and four laden pack ponies, though it turned out that the two men needed to travel well separated as the animals were ungovernable in Varro's presence.

Five times Andada came north with further supplies. By their last meeting Varro was half again the size of an ox and walking on all fours. His neck had begun to fledge and his wings were almost full grown. For Andada's benefit he managed a clumsy flutter of about forty paces. Andada laughed with streaming eyes, but wept very differently as they said good-bye, though Varro told him, speaking with a marked screech in his voice, that he was content with his fate.

It must have been over a year later that Prince Fo, out hunting, was watching an austringer being flogged to death because a hawk had failed to return to the lure. Naturally his entourage were also intent on the spectacle, since it was unwise to be noticed inattentive to the Prince's pleasures, so it was only when the austringer's cries were drowned by a wilder scream that anyone looked overhead. By then the monster was plummeting down with a falcon's stoop. Prince Fo was snatched from his saddle and carried skyward, screaming himself. The monster swung, poised as if having chosen its spot, and dropped him. By the time his company were running towards the outcrop onto which his body had splattered, the monster had swooped again and was carrying the austringer away.

In that same year a strange little man arrived in Timbuktu, black and hideous, but leading two mules laden with expensive and exotic goods. He seemed to know which merchants were reputed to be honest and through an interpreter explained that he had discovered an ancient trade route across the desert and was anxious to reopen it. He didn't want to travel it himself, because he was by nature a stay-at-home, but would like to act as an intermediary and facilitator in his home city for merchants from the north. He had brought samples to show what was available from there, and gold for anything extra that he might buy at the northern end. Because of the scantness of the watering places, his could never be a major route, but for small and costly items such as he had brought it was so much shorter than the long circuit round the desert that it was well worth while.

All this seemed straightforward enough, and worth further investigation. Only two things he said raised eyebrows. When he was asked about the security of the route, and how many guards would be needed, he laughed and said it was unnecessary. That might have been foolhardiness, though the little man seemed sensible enough in other ways, but what were his hearers to make of his explanation that only one fee would be demanded for use of the route—a young and healthy slave, to be left for the demon that guarded the fourth and best watering place? Still, unless remarkably handsome, untrained slaves were two a penny in the market, and the little man was evidently serious for he went and bought three on the morning of his departure, explaining that one was his own fee and the other two were for the two men the merchants had hired to go with him and return with a report on the route.

Word of the expedition must have reached ears other than those for which it was intended, for they were followed into the desert by a party of brigands, expecting to overtake and rob and possibly kill them once they were beyond help. The bodies of these men were found two days later piled against the south gate of the city, apparently dead from the mauling of some large beast. The scouts returned to report that on the little man's instructions they had left the slaves tied to a rusty old ringbolt set into the masonry of a ruined temple beside the demon's pool, but had found all three gone on their return; that the route was possible for small parties, well-guided; and the city at the further end was the same as that they already knew from the longer route, and well worth trading with.

Travellers began to pass to and fro. They never saw the demon, though the slaves they left for it were invariably gone without trace by the time they returned. It was assumed that the demon had carried them elsewhere to consume. Other evidence of the demon's existence accumulated. No brigand survived any attempt to rob the merchants. Moreover, occasional travellers who had missed the route in a sandstorm, and given themselves up to die in the desert, woke to find themselves back at the pool with a cache of sun-dried meat under a small cairn by their side. The demon clearly guarded his route well, so much so that in gratitude masons were eventually sent from Timbuktu to rebuild and renovate his temple.

Andada flourished, becoming immensely wealthy and acquiring several more wives and children. He did not trade along the route himself, but once a year, despite his increasing girth, he would have himself carried up into the desert, left there overnight in his litter, and fetched back next day. In his old age, knowing he would never make another such journey, he took his eldest grandson with him, having made the young man vow to repeat the trip each year but tell no one, ever, what he found there. The route remained active on these terms for several hundred years, until suppressed by a puritanical Sultan of Timbuktu who refused to countenance pacts with demons.

Centuries later, the great Victorian explorer, Sir Pauncefoot Smethers, mapping the pitilessly barren ranges near the eastern edge of the desert, found an anomalous fertile valley, uninhabited now but apparently once intensively cultivated, with every slope neatly terraced to catch the seasonal rains, and great cisterns for water storage against drought years. But there was no sign of any city such as would have excited the interests of the archaeologists of those days, so it was another hundred years before any came to enquire further. They were baffled by what they found.

Digging in middens they unearthed plenty of scraps and shards, mainly more or less crudely made from local materials but in a surprising number of styles, with parallels in the ware of places as far away as Armenia and Germany, but with a frequently recurring motif of a winged quadruped with the head of a bird. These could be dated on both stylistic and scientific grounds to any time from the start of the Christian era to around 1200 AD. In addition to these the trowels turned up a considerable number of small luxury items, all ultimately traceable as trade goods that might have passed through the ancient city of Dassun, long ago buried by the desert but even in its prime nine hundred untravellable miles away west.

As if that was not enough of a problem, one of the party, a birdwatcher, scanning the cliffs through binoculars at a time when the slant evening light picked out every detail of the surface, saw a strange carving on a stretch of sheer rock face. It was the outline of a man, five times life size—or rather of a god, for the iconography was clear, the brimmed helmet, the wand of healing, the winged boots. Mercury, or possibly Hermes, if the thing had been of Greek origin. Even the conventional half-smile of the god was discernible with good glasses. But the image had been carved with a technique unknown in the classical world, as far as anyone in the party could remember, every detail gouged into the rock with four parallel lines, as if carved with a four-pointed tool.

The inscription was on a surface at a different angle, not lit by the revealing light of sunset, and so was not noticed until later, by a young woman scanning the rock around the carving for some sign of how it might have got there. The two words, being in Latin, cleared up the question whether the work was Greek or Roman, but otherwise added further dimensions to the riddle. They were carved in yard-high letters using the same four-line technique as in the image of the god and read simply:

MEMENTO VARRONEM

Remember Varro.

# Scops

*TIME: a dozen or so centuries ago, when there was still a Christian Emperor in Byzantium.*
*PLACE: One of the several hundred little islands that were part of his Empire, though it is doubtful whether he had ever given this one a thought.*
*ACTION: A young man is throwing up.*

YANNI WAS DRUNK, BEWILDERED, MISERABLE, lost in the pitch-black dark, shuddering and gasping. All he knew was that he was leaning forward, propping himself against the square edge of something stone, having just vomited everything out of his stomach in one reeking gush into the gap between his legs and the something.

A blinding glare. Immediately on top of it a deafening blast of sound. Lightning and thunder, he woozily recognised.

Two senses blasted away. Now there were only the taste and stink of his own vomit, and the touch of the stone something.

And a memory. In that instant of glare, the stone surface, flat as a table. On it a small, round, fluffy ball.

He straightened a little and gently swept a quivering hand across the top of the something. There. Even more gently, he eased his trembling fingers round the soft ball and picked it up. It squirmed slightly in his grasp but didn't struggle. Through the diminishing fuzz of his deafness he heard a faint cheeping. Yes, he thought that was what he'd seen. A baby bird.

He straightened fully and cupped it carefully between both hands. It squirmed again. By feel he was able to tell what it wanted, so he loosened his grasp, allowing it to work its head between his thumbs. Once there it was still.

Carefully he established control over his balance and looked around. He had come to this place groping through the blind, pitch dark, but now to his surprise, though the cloud cover was dense and low and the thin moon must have long set, there seemed to be enough light for him to recognise where he was. The shapes were strangely fuzzy. He assumed that must be something to do with the wine—he'd never been drunk before—but there was no mistaking the tall pillars either side of him and the lintel above. This was the House of the Wise One. The thing he'd been leaning against while he vomited was the Bloodstone. And on a new-moon night, almost!

In a panic like that of nightmares he stumbled out between the pillars and down through the olive trees. Even under the unthinned olives—nobody tended or harvested the trees that had belonged once to the Wise One—there was enough light for him not to bump into their trunks. With a sigh of relief he turned up the path. As he did so it started to rain, a few huge drops, and then the longed-for downpour. The air filled with the smell of water on parched ground, more glorious even than the smell of fresh-baked bread. Carefully he shifted his grip until he could hold the bird one-handed and tuck it up under his smock, out of the wet. Hunching his body over it for further protection he hurried up the path. The night was now pitch dark again, but his legs knew the way. He wondered how, even drunk, they could have strayed from it.

The rain sluiced down. For himself he didn't mind the drenching. His body was almost like part of the hillside, welcoming wetness. Besides, combined with the sudden bout of panic, the rain seemed to have cleared the fumes out of his head and now he could remember the horrible day, feeling from first light as if the island had a curse on it—heavy, dense air, sunless but oven-hot under the low clouds, tense with thunder that never did more than rumble overhead, while, as if to embody the curse, dark columns of desperately needed rain could be seen falling uselessly far out at sea, or sometimes coming nearer but then sidling past the steep fields and vineyards and tinder-dry scrubland, all dying from the unseasonal spring drought.

In that heat and oppression Yanni and his sister Euphanie had worked all morning in their terraced vineyard, Yanni checking over and repairing the trellises that supported the vines while Euphanie trained and tied in the fresh spring growth that would carry the grapes, and thinned out the unwanted shoots. They had rested unresting through the midday torpor, and returned to work. By the time Yanni had finished in the trellises and joined his sister, the thundery tension had given her one of her headaches, so sour that she could barely see for the pain of it. Despite that, she had kept getting further and further ahead along her own row, and then coming back to find what was holding him up.

"What on earth is the problem now? Oh, Mother of God, Yanni, what have you been up to? There must have been a better lead growth. Don't tell me . . . Yes, here. Your knife slipped, I suppose. And then you've left three side shoots almost on top of each other. Where've you put your brain? Why does it always seem to be somewhere else when I need you to give me a hand?"

And in the end, "Yanni, I simply can't stand this any longer! Go home! Go down to the tavern and tell the others what a stupid, useless great baby you are. Men are the most useless of the Good Lord's inventions, and you're the most useless of men! Or will be, if you ever grow up enough to *be* a man! Go on! There's money in the pot. Take enough for one mug, if you can count that far! Oh, go away! I'm sick of the sight of you!"

So, weeping with shame and anger and frustration, he had done what she had told him and taken the money and gone down to the tavern, and had had a horrible time there too. Usually the men just ignored him, but to night . . .

He pulled himself together and refused to think about it.

As he reached the cottage the door opened. Euphanie stood in the doorway, black against the lamp glow, about to toss something out into the dark. She halted the action and peered.

"Yanni? Are you all right? You must be soaked. Get inside. What happened to you?"

"All right now. Only wet. I went to the tavern. The men don't really want me there, you know. Mostly they ignore me, but to-night they decided to get me drunk. I didn't realise. I thought they were just being friendly at last. Then they threw me out for not standing my round. I'd told them I couldn't, but . . ."

"Bastards! Always trying to beat each other. I don't know what to do. You've got to learn somehow how to deal with them. It's so much easier for women . . . Anyway, I shouldn't have talked to you like that, whatever sort of a mess you were making. I'm sorry."

"It was your head. How's it feel now?"

"Much better. Gone. Like magic. The moment the first drops fell. What've you got there?"

"Look."

He brought his hand out, moved to the lamp and cradled the fluffy scrap of life between his palms. It gaped up at them, blinking, apparently unalarmed. Euphanie craned over and studied it.

"A little scops owl, I think," she said. "Where did you find it?"

"In the House of the Wise One."

"You went there! And on a new-moon night, almost! Are you crazy?"

"I don't know how I got there. I was drunk, remember. I'd no idea where I was. It was blind dark and I just finished throwing up and there was a flash of lightning and I saw this bird. It was only afterwards that I realised I was in the House, and I'd been leaning on the Bloodstone to throw up. Look, it's hungry, what do owls eat?"

"Mice and voles and beetles and things," she muttered, not thinking about it. "They swallow them when they're hunting and cough them up for the babies when they get back to the nest."

And then, after a pause, and more slowly, but still in a hushed voice, "Yanni, the owl, the scops owl, is the Wise One's own bird. I think she brought you to her House. I think you were meant to find it. And look."

She showed him the thing she had been about to throw into the dark when he had come home. It was a dead mouse, one the cat must have brought in, as it often did.

Yanni loved and admired his sister. She was five years older than he was, and since their mother had died seven years ago she had looked after him, as well as doing most of the work on their smallholding, far up the mountain called Crow Castle. He had no memory of his father, who had left the island soon after Yanni was born, telling only a few friends that he was going—but not his wife, because she might have talked him out of it. She was a strong woman, and had managed almost as well (better, some people said) without him. Euphanie was of the same sort, whereas Yanni himself, he guessed, was more like his father. His one determination in an otherwise unfocussed existence was that he would somehow learn to be different.

He waited till Euphanie had lined a small bowl with bits of rag and then settled the owl into it. Determined, this once, to do something right, he sharpened a knife and with still-trembling fingers skinned and gutted the mouse, filleted out the larger bones and chopped up what was left. Not good enough, he decided. He didn't think he could actually swallow and regurgitate the food, but he spooned some of it into his mouth, chewed it up bones and all, spat the mess into his palm, took a morsel between finger and thumb and eased it into the gaping beak. The owl simply looked at him, waiting, so with the tip of his little finger he poked the mess as far as he could down the gullet. Now the owl closed its eyes and its beak and with a look of extraordinary blissful smugness gulped the mess down and gaped again. When it had eaten all his first chewings he repeated the process. Euphanie, normally fastidious about everything they ate, watched without protest.

"Do you think it will live?" he asked her.

"If the Wise One sent it," she said, broodingly. "Yanni, Nana Procephalos kept an owl."

"Lots of people do."

"Not any longer. Not since . . . Yanni, don't tell anyone you've got it. If they find out, don't tell them where you found it. Say the cat brought it in."

Yanni was scared. Scared by what she said. Scared by her tone.

"I . . . I could take it back."

"Not now we've got it . . . seeing how it came."

While he finished feeding the owl Euphanie reheated the supper she'd prepared. It was well after their normal bedtime when they sat down to eat. Yanni chewed without noticing the food. He was thinking about Nana Procephalos, and what had been done to her.

Until a summer ago the island priest had been a cheery, easy-going old man, who had understood the islanders well and been much loved by them. But then, just as he was about to celebrate Eucharist, a dreadful thing had happened. Helped by a visiting priest he had tottered up the steps of the church and turned to bless his parishioners, who were waiting to follow him into the service, that being the custom of the island. At that moment, in front of everyone, he had had some kind of a seizure. His body had convulsed, he had thrown up his arms and given a strange bellowing cry. His face had contorted and gone almost black, and he would have tumbled forward down the steps if the other priest hadn't caught him and lowered him to the ground.

Everyone had watched in horrified silence while the priest had knelt by his side, feeling his pulse, and at last looked up and pronounced the old man dead.

"I will conduct a shortened version of the Eucharist," he had announced, "and we will pray for the good man's soul. After that I will write to the bishop telling him what has happened, and then, if you wish, I will remain on the island until a new priest is appointed."

So it had all been done, until letters arrived from the bishop confirming the visiting priest in his post on a more permanent basis, apparently as much to his surprise as everyone else's.

His name was Papa Archangelos. He was quite a change, not yet forty, but still a stern, imposing figure, forceful and determined. People wondered why he should have accepted a job in such a backwater. Perhaps the bishop felt that the island needed to be shaken out of its torpor. But he had thrown himself into the task. Within a few months he had visited every household on the island, saying he wanted to get to know his flock, and them him. There was far more of the former than the latter. He asked many questions in a quiet, confiding voice, and listened so sympathetically that even the suspicious islanders tended to tell him secrets that they had long hidden from their neighbours. They learnt almost nothing about him in return, except that he had grown tired of the city and longed for the sea, and the peace to write a great medical book that he had in his head.

He had come late to the remoteness of Crow Castle, but didn't seem to have wearied of his task. He had grieved for Euphanie and Yanni over the loss of both parents, and promised to see if he could confirm the rumour of their father's death. He had praised Euphanie for her courage in running the smallholding, and caring for Yanni like a mother, when she herself was hardly out of her childhood. He wondered how they would manage, so far from help, should one of them fall ill, told Euphanie some remedies for common ailments, and asked her for any herbal lore she had learnt from her mother before she died. For his book, he had said. Euphanie had told him the few things she knew, and added that really for that he should talk to Nana Procephalos.

"So I hear," he had said, smiling. "But she is strangely secretive."

They had stood at the gate and watched him stride away down the hill.

"Too good to be true," Euphanie had muttered.

"I didn't like him either," Yanni had answered. "I don't know why."

"We'd better start going to church every Sunday from now on. In case he notices we're not there. . . I wish I hadn't told him about Nana."

"It sounds as if a lot of other people did too."

"I'm afraid so."

Three months later a special court, sent by the bishop from the mainland, had found Nana Procephalos guilty of witchcraft and sentenced her to death by stoning. The evidence seemed incontrovertible. Spies, also from the mainland, had kept watch on her, followed her one new-moon night, and caught her in the House of the Wise One, in the act of sacrificing a black cockerel on the Bloodstone. So by order of the bishop she died in that place, under a hail of rocks.

Papa Archangelos had let it be known, in his sermon before the stoning, that those who refused to attend it would lay themselves open to suspicion of sympathy with witchcraft. A few of the islanders had contrived excuses, Euphanie among them, saying that Yanni was ill and she had to nurse him. But most had gone. Some of the men had joined in the stoning, whooping as the rocks went home. For several weeks after they continued to boast in the tavern of what they'd done.

Now the islanders learnt that rumours had reached the bishop of witchcraft being rife on the island, and that Papa Archangelos had been originally sent to investigate, and then confirmed in his post to destroy this nest of evil. Too late the islanders began to regret some of the things they had told him. But all, like Euphanie and Yanni, became regular churchgoers, and those who had failed to attend the stoning became very careful of what they said and did.

So from the very beginning Yanni and Euphanie did their best to see that there was no trace of the owl's presence. Islanders tended not to name their domestic animals. The cat was simply "the cat." But in case they were at some point overheard they decided to name the owl, and since they didn't know whether it was male or female, for the time being they called it Scops, a name that somehow stuck after she'd laid her first egg. That was much later.

Yanni looked after her. Normally slapdash and forgetful, he was as careful about her as Euphanie would have been. Her habits made his task easier. Until she fledged she lived in the bottom of a large earthenware jar at the back of a shelf in the barn with a bit of fishing net tossed carelessly over it in case the cat took an interest, though it showed no sign of doing so. In fact it played an active part in the task. Next time it brought a mouse in Euphanie rewarded it with a scrap of the fish she was cooking, and after that had happened a couple of times more it seemed to get the idea and kept up a steady flow of owl food.

Scops woke at dusk, shrilly demanding to be fed, and Yanni would cram chewed mouse into the gaping mouth until she turned her head away and with a quick, gulping shudder excreted neatly over the side of her nest into the bottom of the jar. Then he would move her, nest and all, into a smaller bowl which he carried into the house and set on the table beside him so that he could feed her chewings of what he was eating, his ears pricked for the rattle of the chain that fastened the gate at the top of the steep path. Every few evenings he practised the drill of whisking her into the old bread oven and piling against it the logs he kept ready beside it. In the end he could do this to a count of eight, whereas he always fastened the gate in such a way that even in daylight it took a count of fourteen to unwrap the chain and reach the door. The need never arose, but it was a way of reminding himself to be careful.

Scops spent the night in the oven with the door a crack ajar, and at first light was already calling for food. Never in his life had Yanni regularly risen so early. He fed her before he breakfasted and took her out to the barn when he and Euphanie set off for their day's work.

In two weeks she had doubled her size, and the same two weeks later. By then she had learnt to scrabble out of her bowl and explore round the table while they ate. Already she was moulting her baby down and the quills of her first true feathers were poking through what was left. Her head could swivel through a complete circle in either direction, so that if she happened to be looking Yanni's way when she stretched and flapped her skimpy wings, her large-eyed owl stare gave her an expression of utter bafflement that they hadn't done their job and carried her into the air.

Mobility made the problem of her droppings much more difficult. Birds, Euphanie said, were untrainable, so Yanni watched her every instant she was loose, at first with a damp cloth ready to hand. Soon though he learnt the almost imperceptible signal and if he was quick enough could catch the splatter directly onto the cloth. He applied the same vigilance to all her leavings, the moulted feathers, the little pellets of mouse bones she would from time to time cough up, and so on.

"You are getting even more fussy than me," said Euphanie, teasing.

"Going to church helps," said Yanni, dead serious. "Seeing him again, week after week. He's not going to give up."

By now it was high summer. The spring rains had been kindly, almost healing the ravages of last year's drought. Between the dew-sweet dawns and the dusty cool of the evenings the island seemed to drowse its days away, purring gently as it slept. But it was not at peace. Papa Archangelos was a disturbing priest. People didn't know what to expect when they saw the tall black figure pacing towards them along one of the network of tracks that crisscrossed the island. True to his promise he knew everyone in his flock by now, not only their names but their hopes and troubles, and their place in the complex kinships that, rather like those connecting tracks, linked the community together. On meeting he would bless you, and ask a few friendly seeming questions, bringing himself up to date with your affairs since you had last met him, but as you parted you felt he had seen into your inmost heart. Few of the islanders went to formal confession, and those only once a year, travelling to a priest on another island to do so for greater secrecy. Papa Archangelos put no pressure on his flock to come to him. There was no need. He knew.

He was a wonderful preacher, using images of fishing and farming and housekeeping, things the islanders understood. He spoke of the Lord Jesus as if he had met him and talked with him face-to-face, walking the same earth they did and breathing the same air. But every now and then he spoke of a different Christ, the huge-eyed frowning judge whom they could just make out up in the smoky mosaics in the dome of the church, and to whom they would answer on the day of judgment for every ill deed, every sinful thought, every wicked dream in all their lives. At these times he seemed to grow taller as he spoke, and darker, the soft voice whispering though the breathless stillness until the air in the church felt midwinter cold. More than once someone listening had screamed, or shouted in terror, and rushed out into the sunlight. Yanni needed no other reminders to be careful to keep the existence of Scops a secret.

In fact the house where he lived with Euphanie was the last on a track that led nowhere useful, and Papa Archangelos didn't return there till the grapes were ripe on the vines. By then Scops was flying, and no longer roosted in the jar on the shelf, but on a beam up in the barn, as a wild owl might well do. She slept most of the day, but when he returned with Euphanie from the fields in the evening she would wake at the rattle of the gate and as they reached the door of the house would drift down with her uncanny silent flight, noiseless as a falling leaf, and settle on his shoulder and nibble his ear while he teased the feathers at the back of her neck. Then she would go off and hunt, but not very seriously, knowing she would find food at the house when she returned.

One such evening Papa Archangelos was waiting for them at the gate.

Yanni's heart lost a beat, and another. There was vomit in his throat. But his legs walked on, helpless.

Euphanie knew what to do.

"Take the corn into the barn," she whispered. "Leave it there. Say hello to Scops, then come. He'll be gone before she's finished hunting."

Papa Archangelos raised his hand in blessing as they approached and waited for Euphanie to open the gate. She handed her basket to Yanni, and led the way through. Yanni came last, turning aside with both baskets, and on round the corner of the house to the barn. As he reached for the latch Scops did her silent swoop to his shoulder and nibbled his ear. His panic eased.

"Stay clear till he's gone," he whispered. "We don't want him to see you."

She didn't of course understand the words, but she seemed to sense his tension and slipped away to become part of the gathering dusk. Inside the house he found Papa Archangelos sitting at the table with a jar of wine, bread, and a dish of olives beside him, and Euphanie still standing, opposite. It wasn't the custom of the island for a woman to sit if a man, not a member of the family, was in the room. Papa Archangelos waved Yanni to the other chair, as if this had been his house.

"I cannot stay long," he said. "I have two things to tell you. The first is for you alone, and is sad news. You remember I told you I would try to find whether your father still lived. I have not been wholly successful, but a priest I know in Alexandria tells me there is very good reason to believe that your father died of the plague in that city four years ago. He was working in the docks there when the plague struck and was not among those recorded as having left, and was not seen again. I am sorry, my children. He may not have been a good father to you, but your father he was, nonetheless. Let us pray for his soul."

He rose, so Yanni did the same and stood with his head bowed while the priest whispered three short prayers. In the silence that followed he could hear the throb of his own heart. Something was going to happen. Something . . .

"Thank you, Father," said Euphanie, and Yanni managed to mumble his own thanks.

"The second thing," said Papa Archangelos more briskly, "I am telling everyone on the island. Our blessed Emperor has ordered a census of all his peoples, and soon the census takers will be coming to this island. There is nothing to fear from them, provided you tell them the truth. The penalties for lying are very harsh. You understand."

"Yes, Father, of course," said Euphanie, though he had spoken to Yanni.

They waited for him to go, but he stood gazing down at Yanni. Unable to meet his gaze Yanni looked away and found himself watching the fingers of the priest's right hand as they slowly turned the broad silver ring on the middle finger of his left. He was trapped, hypnotised, by the steady, repetitive movement. Something was going to happen. Something was . . .

"What troubles you, my son?" said the soft voice. "Your father's death?"

"Er, no . . . No . . . I don't . . . don't remember him at all . . . It's all right . . ."

"But there is something?"

*Something? Yes, something . . . Yanni must tell him . . . something . . .*

"It was my fault, Father," said Euphanie. "I made him go down to the tavern to be with the men there. I thought somehow he must learn to be among men, not having a father to help him, you see. They didn't want him there. At first they cut him out but then one night they deliberately got him drunk and then threw him out—because he couldn't stand his round, they said, though he'd told him he couldn't. Now he hasn't got any self-confidence at all."

Yanni had almost fainted with relief as she'd begun to speak. In another few seconds he would have told Papa Archangelos about Scops. But now it was all right. The pressure was gone. Papa Archangelos stood looking down at him, nodding. The reflected lamp light put an orange glint into the dark eyes.

"Yes," he purred. "It can be hard for a young man without a father, and no friends of his own age. But your sister is right, Yanni. You must learn to deal with men. Go to the tavern again. Kosta, I expect, was it, and Thanassi and their cronies? These are not bad men, Yanni, just thoughtless. I will speak to them. It will be all right. And I will see you in church, no doubt. Till then, my friends."

"You've got to go now," said Euphanie, "or he'll think there was something else after all. I'm sorry. It was the best I could think of, before you blurted out about Scops. That's what he wanted."

"Kosta isn't a good man," said Yanni. "Nor's Thanassi. I've heard them talking about what they did to Nana. I don't think some of the others liked it either, but they didn't want to say so. All right, I'll go."

"Sorry about last time, kid," said Kosta, squeezing him by the elbow in greeting. "It was just a bit of fun, right? And everyone's got to get blind drunk once in his life, find out what it's like. After that, the trick is to know what you can hold and stop there."

"I still can't stand my round," said Yanni.

"Never mind that for now," said Thanassi. "When we're old dodderers and you're earning good money, then it'll be your turn."

And the others were as friendly. They made a place for him at their table where he could watch the backgammon, two games being played simultaneously with the rest of the men watching and placing small bets. Kyril, in his ear, explained the intricate skills of the simple-seeming game. He'd brought enough money for a couple of mugs of wine and placed some of it as a bet on Dmitri and doubled his stake when he won. Everyone laughed.

"That rate you'll be standing your round after all," said someone.

"I'll start now," said Yanni and poured his winnings back into their communal jug. They laughed, with him, not at him, though he had a slight feeling that Stavros had deliberately allowed Dmitri to win. And when he rose to go they made no effort to stop him, but waved cheery hands and told him to come back soon.

"You're all right, kid," said Kosta—the same Kosta who had chortled about how he had smashed Nana Procephalos's nose in with a well-aimed rock. How could they be one person? How could even the magical voice of Papa Archangelos have persuaded the old Kosta to change into the new one? He was still thinking about this as he passed the last house along the harbour and turned up the steep track between the olive groves.

With the faintest of whispers Scops settled onto his shoulder and nibbled gently at his ear. He almost laughed aloud in astonishment. She was still a young bird, and he'd never seen her so far from the house before. He must have been twenty paces further on before he realised that the night had grown suddenly less dark. It wasn't that the moon had come out—it was already bright in a clear sky, half full and setting toward the west—but the darkness itself had somehow paled, so that he could see details of the track some distance ahead, and what had been shadowy blank shapes, merely darker than the darkness of night, became solid and fully visible. It was very strange. He hadn't had anything like this happen to him before . . .

Yes he had! That horrible night in the spring, when the men had made him drunk and he'd thrown up on the Bloodstone—that had been pitch dark until he'd started down through the olives with the baby owl cupped between his hands and her head poking out—then it had become almost as light as this, though there had been no moon. Only everything had still seemed much fuzzier than now . . . Yes, of course, because Scops had only had baby eyes and could tell light from dark but couldn't yet see things properly . . . And when it had started to rain and he'd tucked her under his smock, then it had gone dark again, because he'd been seeing things through her eyes and she couldn't see anything in there. He must be doing the same now.

He experimented, and found that he had to be looking in the same direction as Scops for the effect to work. If he turned his head suddenly to his right all he saw was dark until Scops turned her head that way too. The area to his left that was hidden from Scops by his head remained in a triangle of darkness that moved beside him up the track as he climbed.

He didn't have much time to wonder at the strangeness of this. He was just starting on the steepest part of the track when Scops nibbled , or rather pecked, at his ear. Not an owl kiss but a definite peck. The track ahead went dark. Startled, he turned his head and could just make out that Scops had swivelled hers right round and was watching back the way they had come. He slowed his pace and looked back over his shoulder until he could see by owl light what she was seeing.

A man, about fifty paces behind, coming up the track.

Well, why not? Several other families used the lower reaches of this track, and it was not that late. He passed one turning, and then another. The man took neither of them. Well, there was a way to find out. In the shadow of a tree he stopped for a piss he didn't need and looked back, turning his head only far enough to be able to see out of the corner of his eyes, in case the pallor of his face betrayed that that was what he was doing. The man came on another dozen paces, stepping sideways out of one patch of moon shadow into another on the far side of the track. His footfall was noiseless, despite the stony ground. Yanni didn't need the brief interval of moonlight to tell who the burly, pot-bellied figure was.

Stavros. And he had been wearing rope-soled shoes in the tavern. Most of the men wore boots. He was a fisherman, and lived in a shack close to the harbour. There wasn't even a woman up this way he might be visiting. Without owl sight, could he have seen Scops at that distance, perched on Yanni's shoulder? Yanni didn't think so, not even in moonlight. Deliberately he rattled a few pebbles as he moved on. Stavros continued to follow.

For some reason Yanni wasn't really scared. Tense and wary, but with a belief in himself that he wouldn't have had a few months ago. It might only have been the wine, he realised, but in his heart he believed it was something to do with Scops, with the fact that through her he could see in the dark, and perhaps there were other powers he didn't know about yet. And in a way it was a relief to have his doubts about the men in the tavern confirmed, to know that their sudden amazing friendliness wasn't a change of heart, and to guess now that what Papa Archangelos had said to them had had little to do with being nice to fatherless young men. Both were part of some plan. With the help of Scops he would find out what it was, and perhaps outwit them all.

Before they were home Scops slipped away into the night, and he walked the last stretch in the human dark. When he closed the gate he fixed the chain so that it would rattle at a touch, and as soon as he was in through the door put his finger to his lips. Euphanie stared at him. They waited tense. The chain rattled briefly, and stilled as if someone had clamped a hand over it.

"No, it was all right," he said, in slightly too loud a voice. "They were much nicer than last time, and I sat with them and watched them play backgammon. In fact I won a mug of wine on a bet, but I put it back in the jug as part of standing my round. I had a good time. What's for supper? I'm hungry."

"Well, you're going to need to set the table before you can eat," she said, with the same exaggerated audibility. "Anyway, it'll be twenty minutes till it's ready."

"Then I may as well take the trash out."

He left with the bucket by the back door and carried it along the top terrace. As he slung its contents down the slope a horrible thought came to him. Perhaps he'd understood the whole episode wrong. Perhaps it wasn't him that Stavros was interested in, but Euphanie—a lone young woman living with her weakling brother far from any other dwelling—a brother who now thought he could trust these friends . . .

He turned to hurry back to the house, but Scops whispered down onto his shoulder. Now, by owl light, he could see Stavros standing in the shadow of the lemon tree, with his ear pressed to the kitchen shutter.

Scops slipped away almost at once. Yanni walked back with the heavy iron bucket hanging loose in his hand ready to be swung as a weapon against an attacker, and passed within six feet of the intruder, who made no move. Once in he bolted both doors, something they never normally troubled with, and he and Euphanie then discussed tomorrow's tasks in the intervals of eating, until they heard the scratch of Scops's beak on the shutter by which Stavros had been standing, and the soft *prrp, prrp* of her call, and knew that the watcher had left. He let the owl in and she sat on his shoulder while in a low voice he told Euphanie everything that had happened.

"This is the priest's doing," she said. "Who can we turn to? Mother of God, who can we trust?"

"Nobody. Only ourselves. And Scops."

"What can we do?"

"Watch, listen. Bolt the doors at night, and when I go to the tavern."

"You're going again?"

"It's the only way we can find anything out. They'll start asking me to do something soon, to join them in something, I don't know what. We'll know a bit more then."

She nodded, frowning. It was strange that he should be the one taking the lead, and that he should accept it, but that was how it seemed to be at the moment, for both of them.

The moon grew to its full, and waned. Yanni went each Tuesday to the tavern. The men were as friendly as before, and one of them played a board of backgammon with him, giving him odds of two free tiles, and then only one, as he learnt the game. To his surprise he found himself understanding its mathematical subtleties far better than he would have a few months back, when that kind of thing merely had the effect of making his mind go blank. Indeed on the third evening he beat Dmitri fair and square, without needing to use his free tile.

"Pretty good, kid," said Kosta. "That makes you one of us, now."

The others laughed, but with a note in their laughter that suggested there was more than one meaning to the joke. Otherwise he learnt no more.

On the first of those evenings nobody followed him. Scops met him just outside the town as before, and sat on his shoulder the whole way home. On the second Tuesday there was no sign of Scops until she drifted out of the dark when he was already well started on the climb, and then nestled close against his head. Just before the track bent sharply back on itself to tackle a steeper stretch she bit his lobe in warning and at once slipped away. Yanni climbed on, suddenly tense. A tall cypress stood in the crook of the corner, with an olive close against its further side. Between the two trees was a pitch-black cavern.

Yanni stopped, knelt, and probed with a finger into the back of his boot, as if easing out a pebble that had slipped in there. The change of angle brought into view a patch of starlit hillside beyond the trees. Silhouetted against it was the shape of a man. He couldn't tell who it was, but Thanassi had left the tavern early.

He rose and climbed on. The man didn't try to follow him, and Scops rejoined him further up the slope.

"See you Tuesday," he said as he left after the third evening.

"Make it Thursday," said Kosta. "Tuesday's a new-moon night. Tavern's closed."

"Oh, yes, of course," he said.

Nobody left home on new-moon night, if it could be helped, certainly not just to go to the tavern. So they might as well close.

He wasn't followed home. And still he had learnt nothing new, worth knowing.

He started to sleep badly, falling off almost before he lay down but then waking only two or three hours later and lying through the small hours, tense with the inner certainty that events were moving towards some climax while he had no way of knowing what it would be or when it would happen. New-moon night came, and he woke as usual. No, even earlier than usual. Something had woken him. It came again, a scratching at his shutter and a gentle *prrp, prrp.* This had never happened before, not at his bedroom window or this hour. He rose and opened the shutter and Scops was there. She didn't greet him as usual, but simply turned herself round and sat peering out at the night. Nor did she respond to his touch, but instead half spread her wings and leaned forward as if to launch herself out, then stopped the movement and turned her head to look at him.

"You want me to come out?" he whispered. "On a new-moon night? And it's almost midnight."

"*Prrp,*" she said.

Well, why not? He wasn't going to sleep, and as for it being new-moon night, if Scops was there . . .

He rose, found his clothes by touch, dressed, picked up his boots, and went to the back door. There he hesitated whether to tell Euphanie what he was doing, but no sound came from her room and he decided against it. Perhaps he'd only be ten minutes or so . . .

Still on stockinged feet he climbed the path. Scops was waiting for him on the gatepost. Carefully he undid the chain, and knelt to put on his boots. Scops slipped onto his shoulder as he rose.

"Where to now?" he asked.

She told him simply by gazing down the track, which had the effect of casting a beam of owl light along it, so he headed as if for the harbour. But halfway there she turned her gaze aside and directed him into a goat track that led him up an outlying spur of the central mountain of the island. Twice she left him to stand in the dark while she prospected for paths through the scrub along which he would be able to walk. They crossed the ridge and headed down beside a remnant of the old forest that had once covered the island, but had been felled to build the galleys of the Romans. They followed a stream downhill, turned aside yet again for short climb, crossed a lesser ridge and halted.

Ahead, black as the pupil of an eye, lay the sea. Nearer, with a few lights showing round the harbour, the crinkled shoreline of the island. Nearer still, immediately down the plunging slope, the House of the Wise One, invisible in its own natural bowl from anywhere but the hillside where he stood.

The glow of a small fire lit the space between the pillars, and grotesque shapes, small with distance, were moving around it. But for the owl light he couldn't have known they were there except when they passed directly between him and the fire. He stared. A sudden chill had wrapped him round, though the night was warm for October. Demons, woken by the New Moon to dance in the House of the Wise One? They were animal-headed, as demons might be, though the heads seemed large for the bodies, and they stood on their hind legs and the bodies were human or part-human. Not animals, then. Humans . . .? A shape, a known shape, strutted past the flames. Stavros, with the head of a horse covering the upper part of his face and a horse-tail swinging behind. And the one with the limp must be Thanassi, and the skinny one old Dmitri. Yanni numbered the others off. They were all there, and at least four more, two of whom looked as if they might be women.

A white goat was tethered to a pillar at the end of the temple opposite the Bloodstone. It paid no attention to the dancers, but stood with its head bowed, as if it had fallen asleep.

At first the dancers simply circled the fire with slow, prancing steps, but soon they began to dance more vigorously, leaping and stamping their feet, and throwing their masked heads violently back and forth. He could hear faint whoops and cries.

The dance went on for a long while. The pace quickened and quickened. They should have been utterly exhausted by now, but they didn't seem to tire. And then, suddenly, they halted and turned towards the far end of the temple, where the goat was tethered. A gap opened on that side of the circle.

Out of the darkness beyond the pillars paced a new figure, naked apart from a short leather skirt. The mask was that of a bull and, unlike those of the dancers, covered the whole head. The body was a man's body, but half again as tall as any of the dancers. Flesh and hide were the colour of polished brass, and glinted like brass in the light of the fire. In his right hand the newcomer carried a flat dish with a few small objects on it. The dancers greeted him with a wild yodelling call, so loud that it carried clearly up to where Yanni and Scops watched. They crowded round him with upraised arms, and then fell back. There was a long pause. Nobody moved. When at last the Bull-man stepped forward, the others restarted their dance, slowly circling him and moving with him as he paced up to the fire.

Here he halted again, took something from the dish, and with a sower's gesture sprinkled it onto the fire, which instantly flared up into a white blaze, that died almost as quickly away. When it was gone the whole space between the pillars was filled with a dull red glow that didn't fade like the flames, but persisted, unchanged. Compared with the owl light of the dark beyond, Yanni could now see everything within the temple as clearly as he might have done in an early dusk. He watched the Bull-man pace round the fire and on up the temple towards the Bloodstone, the dancers moving with him, circling faster and faster, dancing themselves into a renewed frenzy, their repeated calls echoing up the hillside. The

Bull-man reached and rounded the Bloodstone. He laid the dish down on it, turned to face the fire and stood still.

Two of the dancers, the ones Yanni thought were Dmitri and Thanassi, broke from the wheeling circle, pranced back down the temple, unleashed the goat, tipped it, unresisting, onto its side, lifted it by its legs, ran back up the temple and swung it up onto the Bloodstone, where they stretched it out and held it down. It made no effort at all to struggle or free itself.

The Bull-man picked up a flask from the dish and with a steady, ritual movement poured something into a bowl. He put the flask back on the dish and picked up what looked like a knife or dagger, paused again, and raised his head and arms towards the stars. The blade of his dagger glinted orange in the red light.

He opened his great bull mouth. The dancers reeled back. A moment later Yanni heard the thunder of his bellow, shaking the hillside. He seemed to have grown even larger, now twice the size of any of the dancers. Yanni stared at him openmouthed. He had seen the huge muscles of the neck flex. He had seen the mouth open. And that roar could not have come from any human lungs. The creature's head was no mask. It was his own.

The dagger flashed down. The dancers screamed again. The Bull-man laid the dagger aside, lifted the goat's head by one horn and held it clear of the slab, and with his other hand took the cup and held it so that the blood streamed into the bowl. The bowl steamed. He dropped the goat's head, gripped the bowl by its stem and raised it towards the sky. The screams grew louder, shriller. He lowered the bowl to his mouth and drank. Still screaming the dancers rushed forward. He flung what was left in the bowl over them, and they fought to lick it from each other's bodies until he tossed the dead goat among them, and then climbed onto the Bloodstone and towered over them while they scrabbled to and fro, a mass of bloody limbs and bodies, fighting like a pack of starving dogs to tear the carcass to pieces with their bare hands and then gnawing at the tatters they had managed to wrench from it, skin, offal and all.

All the time the monstrous figure on the Bloodstone seemed to grow huger.

Yanni watched for a moment, disgust and terror swirling inside him, and turned away.

"Let's go home," he muttered.

He barely noticed how he got to the gate. His legs carried him. Scops showed him the way. He let himself in, woke Euphanie, and sitting in the dark at the end of her bed with Scops still on his shoulder, told her what he had seen. After a little while she climbed out of the sheets, wrapped a blanket round herself and sat beside him, cradling him and he her against the terrors of the dark while he finished his story. She carried her clothes into the kitchen, lit both lamps, and dressed while he sat staring at the tabletop. Every now and then he would remember some detail and mutter it to her. But again and again he returned to the behaviour of the goat, its torpor, the way it didn't struggle or try to escape.

"Goats aren't like that!" he said

"They'd drugged it?" Euphanie suggested.

"I suppose so."

Neither wanted—neither dared—to go back to their rooms and lie in the dark, alone, so to get themselves through the small hours Yanni scrubbed the floor and cleaned the stove and Euphanie went through all her cupboards, sorting out her stores, reminding herself of what she had and what she still needed to lay in for the winter. Together they cleared the shelves and cleaned all they had, down to the smallest egg-cup. By dawn the kitchen was spotless.

This was just as well, because soon after sunrise they heard the rattle of the gate. Scops flew up onto a beam and tucked herself out of sight, and with a sick feeling and a thundering heart Yanni opened to door to see who had come.

Three men and a woman, none of them islanders, stood on the track. Two of the men were some sort of servants, carrying bundles of rolled parchment. The third, by his dress, was an official. He took a roll from one of the others, opened it and came down the path, running a finger down a list and stopping at a line.

"The Philippes holding?" he asked. "The previous census, twenty-two years ago, listed one man, one woman, and one infant daughter."

"Oh . . .well . . . my father and mother are dead," said Yanni, stammering with relief. "The baby must have been my sister. I was born after the census. I'm Yanni Philippes."

"Excellent. I will record the household details later. But now, while the day is still cool, I will go round your holding and recheck the boundaries, and you can tell me of any changes in the nature of the holding since the previous census."

"My sister had better do that," said Yanni. "She knows much more about it than I do."

The official frowned—Yanni was a man, and therefore legally the master of the household—but nodded and turned to the two servants to sort out the rolls he would need. The woman came drifting past them, unnoticed.

"May I come in?" she said in a soft voice. "I like to travel, so I come with my brother on these tours, but now I am tired from the climb and would like to rest."

Yanni stood aside to let her pass. Euphanie had been listening just inside. The woman acknowledged her curtsey with a smiling nod. She was short and plump, grey-haired, and wore a soft grey travelling cloak clasped at the neck with an ivory brooch carved with the head of a woman who had a tangle of writhing serpents instead of hair.

"You must go with my brother," she told Euphanie. "Check the clerks' work, every line. Sometimes they have been known to cheat, and acquire land for themselves."

Euphanie curtseyed again and left. As soon as the door closed behind her, Scops glided down and settled on the visitor's wrist. The visitor seemed to change, but not in any way Yanni could have put words to. Her eyes were very strange, both grey and green, not a mixture of those two colours nor one flecked with the other, but a clear soft grey and a soft olive green, both at the same time. The kitchen throbbed with her presence.

Realising whose presence that was, Yanni fell to his knees.

"Help us, please help us!" he gasped.

"That is why I have come," said the woman. "May I sit here? And you in your own chair. But first, if you will, bring me some water, and a corner of your sister's last baking, and a little of your oil. Don't be afraid of me, Yanni. I have very little power. What you are looking at is no more than the ghost of a god, lingering on in a place where she was once loved and feared. My thanks."

She passed her free hand over the loaf he had brought and broke off a corner, and laid two fingers briefly on the oil flask before pouring a little oil into the dish he had put in front of her. She dipped her bread into the oil, let it soak a few seconds, and ate, chewing like any ordinary woman. It was bad manners on the island not to share the food you offered to your guest, so hesitantly Yanni took a little for himself. The terrible night had left his mouth sour and dry. He wouldn't have thought he could taste anything, but instantly his palate cleared, and he realised that he would never again eat bread so light, so flavourful, so crisp-crusted, so soft inside, nor oil so subtly sweet.

The goddess smiled.

"I still have a few small powers," she said. "Now, about why I have come. I saw what you saw last night through the eyes of Scops, and I will tell you what it meant. There have always been forces, powers, energies—but there are no words for them because they do not participate in the dimensions of time and space, so that even the word 'always' is wrong for their mode of existence.

But they pervade all universes, all the multiplicity of possible dimensions, and in all of those there is a pressure from these forces to be embodied into the realities of each place. Here in this world, the pressure works through the human imagination. It was people who long ago embodied me into the dimensions of here and now.

"Think of lamplight beaming out into the night from a lit window. Now think, if you can, of the light travelling the other way, beaming in from those shadowy spaces and gathering itself into the central lamp, creating a single intense brightness. That is how people create the gods. They take their faint perceptions of these ungraspable forces and beam them in to a single focus in the here and now, and the god becomes real, and full of the previously unrealised powers of the many, many people who have made it. I am the ghost of such a god, all that is left after people have withdrawn their imaginations from me, apart from a funny little superstition here and there. I can exist as a ghost on this island, partly because no islander would willingly harm a scops owl, though most of them do not know why this is so.

"But the forces from which I and my kind originate are mixed, negative and positive; and the people are mixed too, and embody these differences into darkness and light, joy and grief, hope and despair, love and cruelty. So that is how I and my kind were, mixtures. As I told you, even on this island I was both loved and feared. Now, somehow there has grown up among humans, especially around this inland sea, a longing for oneness, a single source of creation, a single explanation for all the different lesser explanations, a single god. And human reason told them that whereas gods of my kind can be balanced against each other, so that the whimsical caprice of one can be mitigated by the benevolence of another, a single god cannot. A god of my kind is a god as he or she *might* be. But a single god must be as a god *ought* to be, a god of light, and love, and justice. So your new god is embodied by the imaginations of reason to be these things.

"But where are the darker powers to go? People know in their hearts that they are still there, so they embody them by their own dark imaginings. This is what you saw beginning to happen last night, here on my island. I have no power to stop it. I am a puff of smoke in the wind compared to the solidity of this dark god. But you could, and only you, and I can tell you how and give you a few small glamours to help you. It will be very dangerous, and you may not succeed, but you are already in terrible danger. It is your choice, Yanni."

There was only one possible answer.

"I . . . I . . . I'll try."

Twenty-seven days later, though he had gone to bed twanging with nerves, Yanni slept late—a little gift from the goddess, he guessed—and didn't wake until the sun was well up. Euphanie was waiting for him in the kitchen, serious and pale.

"She came to me in my dream," she said. "She told me what you are going to do tonight. Oh, Yanni!"

(Nobody on the island except themselves seemed to have met, or even seen, the census-taker's sister, though the men in the tavern and the women in the market had talked animatedly about the census-taking, and their possible losses or gains from the re-evaluations that were going to result. Euphanie, indeed, had been one of the lucky ones. Following her visitor's advice she had checked every detail in the rolls, and had discovered an error that meant she had been paying excess taxes since the previous census. Rather than face the hassle and litigation of suing for full repayment she had accepted a reasonable sum in settlement on the spot, which was how Yanni had been able to stand his round on his visits to the tavern this last month.

And then to drink his share. Or rather to make it seem as if he had, by practising the glamour the goddess had shown him. It was something like what she had said about the way the gods are embodied, the light streaming in to the central point of the lamp, as it were a willed belief, intense enough to rouse echoes of itself in the minds of others, and then beamed in with them to a central point—a mug, for instance—so that the mug appears to be brim full when it has only a dribble of wine in the bottom. A dozen such dribbles in an evening aren't enough to get a grown man drunk, though Yanni had been apparently reeling by the time he left the tavern each night. He was confident now that he could make it happen again, new-moon night or not.)

It was the new-moon night nearest midwinter, and had been dark for three hours by the time Yanni walked down the hill. Pitch dark now, all stars hidden behind heavy, slow-moving cloud. He carried a lantern, because it would have seemed strange not to do so on such a night. Scops went with him, not riding on his shoulder but slipping invisibly from tree to tree through the olives, or moving further from the track to swoop low across a patch of scrubland or a vineyard, then calling softly when she returned to the track to reassure him that she was still there.

In the pocket of his pouch he carried the odd-shaped piece of wood that the goddess had told him he would need. He had spent some time searching the hillside for exactly the right branch, and had eventually cut it from a wild olive, shaped and smoothed it, and, lying on the kitchen table, with Euphanie's help practised what he planned to do with it.

His palms were sweaty with tension. He felt scared but not terrified. He believed he could face what was coming, and cope with it, provided he kept his wits. And he wouldn't be alone. Scops was already with him, and the goddess would be there, she had told him, and she would bring helpers, each in themselves as near-powerless as she was, but together, perhaps, worth something.

A noise on the path ahead of him, coming from round the next bend. It paused and came again, more prolonged. Footsteps crossing a patch of loose gravel. Several people climbing the path. He drew aside, tucked his lantern under his cloak and waited. He had been half expecting this.

"See you Tuesday, Yanni?" someone had called when he'd been leaving the tavern last week.

"They'll be shut here, won't they? It's a new-moon night again," he'd answered. (He'd been wondering how they were going to manage this.)

"Oh, we'll meet at my place," Kosta had said. "Usual time."

"Long way to walk down on a new-moon night, lad," Stavros had suggested.

"No, I'll be all right," he'd said confidently. "See you at Kosta's, then."

Despite that, they couldn't have been sure he'd not have changed his mind, or been persuaded to by his sister, so now they were coming to unpersuade him, and if necessary to take him by force, and perhaps Euphanie as well.

They rounded the bend, dim shapes in the light of their lanterns, climbing in silence. He couldn't tell them apart until they were almost level with him.

"Stavros?" he called softly.

They stopped dead. Stavros clutched at Dmitri's arm as they turned to face him.

"It's me, Yanni," he said easily. "I didn't mean to make you jump—I was just being careful. New moon night, you know."

They relaxed, but there was still a gruffness in Stavros's voice as he answered.

"Good lad. That's why we thought we'd come and see you down. Now you've saved us the climb. Back we go, lads."

They were all as tense as he was, Yanni realised as they descended the hill, and no wonder. They must understand that they were already trapped in a hideous labyrinth, and tonight they were going to descend a whole level further into its darkness. In their hearts they must be yet more afraid than he was. They didn't have even the ghost of a goddess to help them, only a real and terrible master they must obey.

By island standards Kosta was a wealthy man. He was a boat builder, with three paid hands to help him—Dmitri was one of them—and himself owned two fishing boats. He lived in a house larger than most, a little above the town up a different track from the one that led to Crow Castle. The rest of the men were already there in the kitchen, with Kosta's two bustling sisters bringing them little plates of the usual island snacks to add relish to the wine. Apart from that, the meeting was outwardly no different from any other at the tavern, teasing talk, and small bets on the backgammon, and memories of times past. Inwardly, though, it was utterly different. The air stank with tension and dread, and excited expectation, until Thanassi said "Time you were getting home, Yanni, lad."

The tension wound up another notch, twanging taut. Yanni rose swaying, as if in response to the wine they supposed him to have drunk. Any moment now, he thought.

"Nightcap to see you on your way?" said Kosta, also rising. "Settle the wine and give you sweet dreams? Brandy, everyone?"

It would have been a slap in the face to refuse.

"You won't taste brandy like Kosta's again," said Dmitri, himself too drunk not to chuckle at the hideous joke.

Kosta fetched a dozen small glass goblets and a stone bottle from a shelf. Yanni watched him fill one goblet and push it a little to the side, then fill the rest and not move them. He handed Yanni the first glass and the men passed the rest around among themselves. Yanni concentrated his will, the way the goddess had shown him.

"Well, good luck," he said.

They echoed the toast, and watched him over their goblets as they drank. They saw a flesh-and-blood arm raise a solid glass goblet to his lips, and relaxed as they watched him drain it in three gulps.

"Wow!" he gasped, and staggered against the table by the door, slipping the glamour-hidden goblet, still full of the drugged brandy, out of sight behind the fruit bowl that stood on it.

"Bit much for a young head," said Thanassi. "Maybe we better see him home after all."

They all rose together. Two of them took Yanni by the elbows and led him out through the door. Behind him he could hear a sudden bustle of activity. The masks and costumes, he thought, and timber they'd need for the fire, and so on. An owl called from a tree in the garden, *prrp, prrp.*

How long, he wondered, before the drug would have taken hold? Better give it a few more minutes. But he was already supposed to be drunk, so he stumbled, and swayed against Thanassi, who roughly shoved him upright while Dmitri on the other side yanked him into place. Some of the men had lanterns, but once they were beyond the occasional lit windows of the town the night became very dark. In silence they started up the track to Crow Castle. Yanni let his head droop and his feet begin to drag. The men holding him grunted in satisfaction and shifted their grip so that they were now carrying some of his weight. With mild surprise he discovered that he wasn't merely acting drunk and drugged. Unconsciously he had been using the goddess's glamour actually to be those things, while still inside the half-stupefied young man who was climbing the track there was the true, hidden Yanni controlling the illusion, watching its effect and waiting to act.

Twenty minutes above the town they stopped and closed up. Two of the lantern carriers went to the front and led the way into the half-overgrown track that Yanni, drunk, must have stumbled up that first dreadful night to find the baby Scops. Yes, he thought, all this must have been foreseen by the goddess. Though it wasn't far, it was a stiff climb, and most of them were panting with the effort by the time they emerged from among the olives and saw, faint-lit by lantern light against the utter black beyond, the squat pillars of the House of the Wise One.

The men put down what they'd been carrying. Yanni's two minders switched their grip to let Stavros strip off his cloak, and he was able to slip his hand into the pouch and grasp his bit of olive branch and hold it against his wrist while they pulled the sleeve free. None of the three perceived it.

By now he was giggling almost uncontrollably under the influence of the imaginary drug. They stripped off the rest of his clothes and led him naked into the House. Stavros folded the cloak into a pad, and Dmitri settled him onto it and ran a cord under his arms and lashed him to a pillar.

Dazedly he watched Iorgo and Constantine, already in their costumes, build and light the fire with a spill from one of the lanterns. The timber was bone dry and blazed up almost in an instant. The others came back, costumed and masked. There were several more than had been at Kosta's. At least two of them were women.

The masks changed them all. They were no longer people, nor animals either, but something else. They seemed to move differently, to hold themselves differently, from anything that belonged in the workaday world. The one who had been Nicos sounded a rattle of taps on the little drum hanging from a loop round his neck. The creatures stiffened and waited. The taps began again, became louder, steadied to a thumping double beat, and the creatures began to dance. At first they moved in slow, even steps, circling the fire, but soon the beat quickened to a jerky pulse, somebody double-stamped a foot, someone else whooped, and now they were circling faster, stamping on the ancient flagstones, jerking their heads back and forth, clapping out cross-rhythms, whooping and calling to summon their dark god, while their fantastic flame-cast shadows flickered across the line of pillars beyond them.

Yanni felt his own body beginning to tremble, tense with the urge to rise and join the frenzy. No, he told it, not yet, wait.

The dance went on and on, fiercer, wilder, madder. Rapt in their ecstasy the dancers could not tire. And yet, in an instant, in response to no sign or call, they halted, motionless apart from their heaving lungs.

In that silence the Bull-man stalked into the temple.

He stopped barely a yard from where Yanni was lashed. He was no masked man. He was huge. His shoulders were above the upstretched arms of any of the dancers who came whooping and crowding round him, and then fell back into a ring, silent apart from faint eager whimperings, a pack of dogs waiting to be fed. The firelight rippled across the brass of his body. The shadows in its folds and clefts were black as the new-moon night. He stank of animal essences. The pillars of the temple seemed to pulse and waver with his presence, as if Yanni had been seeing them through rising air.

Everything had changed with his coming. The glamour that had protected Yanni so easily this far with its solid-seeming illusions, giving him an almost contemptuous confidence in his ability to outwit the men, seemed to weaken and thin to a gauzy veil. If the god had glanced down at him it would have melted away. But he would not.

"The power flows into him in the instant of the victim's death," the goddess had said. "To look at the victim before that would be to anticipate that moment, and so dilute its power."

The god paid no more heed to the dancers than he did to Yanni, but stood gazing out above their heads while they waited imploring. At last he took a heavy pace forward, and another, and another. The drum rattled. The dancers reformed their ring and began slowly to circle their god, the circle moving with him as he paced up the temple and stood outlined against the fire. Now they ringed both fire and god.

With a sweep of his arm the god strewed a handful of dark grains onto the flames, and a white blaze flared, too brilliant to look at, and died as quickly away, leaving the space enclosed by the pillars filled with a smoky red glow that seemed to come not from the fire but from the stones of the temple themselves. The air within that space reeked with a heady odour, sickly sweet, dazing the senses.

Yanni concentrated his will and forced it away, at the same time freeing both body and mind from his own illusion of drugged torpor, and became fully alert, himself. He felt the glamour the goddess had given him return, though weakened. Perhaps it would still do, he thought. Provided the brass god did not look at him until the moment came.

As before, the drumbeat quickened, the dancers spun faster and faster, stamping, prancing more and more wildly, whooping and calling, flinging heads and arms, thrashing themselves into a mindless, ferocious ecstasy, an agony of lust for the blood of the coming sacrifice.

The god reached the Bloodstone, stalked round it, turned, laid his dish in front of him and waited, massive, impassive, his great beast eyes glinting orange in the red glare as he stared out over the line of pillars at the darkness beyond. Thanassi and Dmitri broke from the spinning circle and raced back down the temple. Dmitri knelt, gripped Yanni by the ankles and pinned them to the floor. Thanassi untied the rope and reached for his wrists.

Yanni was ready for him, gripping in his right hand the stub of side-branch of the olive he'd cut, so that the short length of the main branch lay directly above his wrist. Though weakened, the illusion held, just, and made it seem to Thanassi that he took hold of the wrist itself, real not simply to his eyesight but to his touch as well, real skin, real flesh and bone against his palm and fingers.

Yanni clung to the side-branch as they lifted him and raced back past the fire. The ring of dancers opened to let them pass, and they swung him up onto the Bloodstone and spread-eagled him in front of their god.

The god had not moved. This was the moment of extreme danger. Though the god might not look at Yanni directly, the illusory wrist that Thanassi held must lie near the edge of his vision, and surely, if he should glance this way . . .

He did not. Through half-closed eyes Yanni watched him take up the flask and pour a dark liquid from it. The bowl was out of Yanni's line of sight. With the same calm slowness the god set the flask back on the dish and started to raise arms and head towards the sky. In his right hand he now held the knife, its bronze blade shaped like a pointed leaf and incised with symbols. Now!

Yanni let go of the olive branch and gently moved his own arm, invisible to Dmitri and Thanassi, down past his body. He found the edge of the dish by touch, reached further and found the stem of the goblet.

He waited. The god grew taller, reaching up, yearning, demanding, summoning. The dancers moaned in their nightmare orgasm. The god opened his vast bull mouth and bellowed. The dancers reeled back and crouched down, hiding their faces. And the little illusion behind which Yanni had been sheltering crumpled away and fell to dust.

The god did not stir as the reverberations of his thunder dwindled away over the harbour.

Dmitri and Thanassi had fallen back with the others, letting go of the victim, but Thanassi had gathered his wits and was lurching back towards the Bloodstone when he realised that there was something unexpected in his grasp. He looked and saw the piece of olive wood. He gave a sudden astonished shout, an ordinary human cry, a crack in the surface of the ritual.

The god glanced down.

It was too soon. "Wait till he is about to strike," the goddess had told Yanni, but the illusion was gone and that moment would not now come. He flung the contents of the goblet into the face of the god and instantly rolled himself aside, dropped, and scuttled away between the stunned and stricken dancers.

Behind him the god screamed. Not in surprise or anger, but in agony, the unimaginable agony of a god.

Yanni reached the darkness beyond the pillars and turned to look. The great brass beast still stood where he had been but something was happening to his face. It was melting, bubbling, falling in golden and burning dribbles onto the naked flesh below.

But Yanni had been forced to act too soon. The god was stricken, but not destroyed.. He mastered his pain. The scream stopped. He drew himself up and began to summon his power back into himself. The melting visage hardened and became a ghastly contortion of a face, with its two huge eyes glaring out of it.

Again Yanni turned to run and again stopped. In front of him, all along the rim of the bowl ran a line of lights. Lanterns. Women's voices began to call "Ululului-*leh.* Ululului-*leh.* Ululului-*leh*". Tall figures appeared on the slope in front of them, shadowy—Yanni could see the gleam of the lanterns through their bodies—an armoured man with a high plumed helmet and shield, a smiling naked woman, another woman, with a hunter's bow in her hand and a quiver at her back, and more. They raised their right hands in a gesture of command, of banishment.

As if by owl sight Yanni could see what was happening, though it was not something he saw with his eyes; but the night seemed to be patterned with threads of power as with their residual memories of what their ancestors had once believed the women invoked the old gods back into momentary existence. The old gods gathered that power into themselves, shaped it to their purposes and passed it on, focussed on a single point, not where the new god stood beside the Bloodstone, but at somewhere in the pitch-black sky above him.

From the temple the new god answered with a bellow, and he was a god with living power, while they were only ghosts of what they had been. For a moment their shapes thinned and wavered, and ripples of weakness ran along the threads of power, tangling its pattern. But the women's calling continued unfaltering, the old gods regathered their strength and the pattern returned, centring itself into a single last illusion, so strong that it ceased to be an illusion and became for a little moment part of the reality of this world, solid as a boulder.

Yanni turned back to the temple to see what it was, but there was nothing, only the blackness of the new-moon night where the threads all came together directly above the Bloodstone, on which the new god was now standing. He seemed even taller than before. His head topped the line of pillars. He too gazed skyward, raising his arms to the sky for a fresh outpouring of his strength.

Out of that sky, sudden as lightning, fell a shape, a blackness, a piece of the night itself. With the neck-breaking thud of a hunting owl as it strikes its prey it hit the god full in the face. Immense wings, wide as the temple itself, beat violently. The god, caught utterly by surprise, tumbled from the Bloodstone, tripped on the prone body of a dancer, staggered and lay flat, while the hooked beak plunged down again and again at the head gripped between the savage talons.

And the god withdrew from the shape he had inhabited and slipped away.

The red light dimmed and died. By its last glimmer Yanni saw the owl rise on silent wings and vanish into the darkness of night.

Suddenly he was aware of his nakedness, and of the women with the lanterns beginning to move down the slope behind him. He scuttled up to the temple, found his clothes, hurried into the darkness beyond the firelight and started to put them on.

The night was full of voices, triumphant, questioning, angry. Somebody was calling his name.

"Yanni! Yanni! Where are you?"

"Euphanie! Here! Euphanie!"

Half-dressed he stumbled towards the light of the fire. She came rushing towards him out of the dark and flung her arms round him.

"You're all right! Oh, you're all right! You did it!"

"I . . . I think so . . . But you . . . How . . .?"

"I couldn't go to bed. She came to me in a waking dream. She said I must come. The same with the other women. She told us what to do. They're catching the men now. I don't know what they'll do to them . . . Oh, Yanni! That . . . that *thing!*"

Still appalled by the vision, she was gazing beyond Yanni into the House of the Wise One to where the dark god had stood. He turned. Nobody had yet dared to pass between the pillars, and the temple was empty. The fire was dying, but by its faint light he could see something lying between beside the Bloodstone where the god had fallen. Surely . . . No, it was too small, a human shape. Pulling on the rest of his clothes he took her lantern and went to look.

The face was a tangled mess of beard and blood. Both eye sockets were bloody pits. The pale, naked torso was streaked with dark runnels where the molten flesh of the god's visage had dribbled down it. On the middle finger of the left hand there was a wide silver ring.

Yes, of course, he thought. In his heart he had known it all along. He went back to Euphanie.

"Papa Archangelos," he told her. "I suppose he chose me because he thought I'd be an easy victim. Like Nana. Let's go home."

"Where's Scops?"

"I don't know."

Lamplight gleamed through the kitchen shutters. The census-taker's sister was waiting for them, with Scops on her wrist. There was a meal on the table, cheese, olives, oil and bread, water and wine, and places set for three.

"All is well," she told them. "We could not have done it without you, nor you without us, nor either without Scops. The dark god will return, but not to this island yet, and meanwhile my blessing is upon it, and upon you two, and yours, for as long as you live.

"We old gods have used our last power, and now we are going, and will not return. The glamour I gave you, Yanni, will go with me. You are better off without it. These things belong to the gods, and destroy mortals who use them too long. Papa Archangelos had been a man, remember, and might have been a great one. Tell no one what has happened apart from your own children."

"I wouldn't anyway. Papa Archangelos may be dead, but that won't stop the church stoning people for witchcraft. And the women who came, they'll all be too scared to do any more than whisper among themselves."

"Good. But remember to tell your children, yours and your sister's. And their children after."

"All right. What about Scops?" he asked.

"Oh, she will stay, and mate and rear young, and die like any other owl. But my blessing is on her too. Go to Yanni, little one. No wait."

She broke bread from the loaf, dipped it in water, and used it as a sponge to wipe a few traces of dark blood from Scops's face-feathers, then raised her arm to kiss the bird farewell. Scops nibbled the tip of her nose affectionately and flipped herself across to Yanni's shoulder.

Yanni turned his head to greet her. When he looked back the goddess was gone.

## EPILOGUE

One late summer afternoon two old people, brother and sister, sat in front of the house where both of them had been born almost a hundred years before. Below them, terrace after terrace, stretched their vines and olive trees, and beyond that a placid sea, with two islands on the horizon, cloudy masses against the bright streaks of sunset. Around them sat, or strolled, or scampered, the enormous gathering of their joint family, sons and daughters and grandchildren, all with their husbands or wives, great-grandchildren, two by now also married, and one great-great-grandchild, the first of all the brood to descend from both brother and sister, for her parents were second cousins. That was why everyone had come to celebrate her naming day. Though several of the husbands and wives had died, none of the direct descendants was missing, for they were a long-lived family and those who had married had done so for love and stayed loving. Many had come from the island, more from other islands nearby, or the mainland, some from far-off cities. There were farmers and fishermen there of course, but also merchants and craftspeople—one of the granddaughters was a famous weaver, whose work hung in palaces and cathedrals—a scholar or two, a judge and two other lawyers, priests, monks and a nun with special dispensations to leave their monasteries—all there for this day.

Now an owl floated out of nowhere, settled on the old man's shoulder and sat blinking at the red sun. The light darkened. Voices became hushed and fell silent, as if a long-hidden knowledge had woken suddenly in the blood they all shared.

"*Prrp, prrp,*" said the owl, and the evening air filled with owls. Owls are territorial birds, and it is rare to see more than two together once they have left the nest for good, but for this evening they appeared to have forgotten their boundaries and eddied in silent swirls above the human gathering.

Now some came lower, and the children raised their arms as the owls swooped and turned among them, and ran in interweaving circles, as if birds and people were taking part in some game or dance whose rules none of them knew but all of them understood. The watching adults clapped out a rhythm and the owls called to and fro.

In the middle of the calling and clapping the owl on the old man's shoulder, the fourteenth Scops of that name and line, called again, "*Prrp, prrp,*" so softly that one would have thought only the two old people could have heard, but one owl broke from the dance and flew towards them. The old man stretched out a shaky arm and the owl settled onto it, a bit clumsily, as she was one of this year's hatch and had not been flying more than a week or two. The woman reached out and the young owl leaned luxuriatingly against her touch as her fingers gentled among her neck feathers.

"Well," said the old woman. "They're all here. Which of them are you going to choose?"

The owl flipped itself up onto the old man's shoulder, scrabbled for a hold and then perched beside the older one, studying the crowd below. It slid away and was lost among the swirling owls. But in less than a minute the dance stilled. The children stood where they were and the birds swung away to perch among the olives, all but one, which hovered for a moment in a blur of soft wings and settled on the shoulder of a nine-year-old girl.

Instantly the bond formed, as the girl put up a hand to stroke the owl and the owl nibbled gently at the girl's ear. The girl was island-born, Euphanie's great-granddaughter, her father a fisherman, hitherto a shy and stammering child. But now, with apparently complete assurance, despite all those watching eyes, she turned and climbed the steps to where the old couple sat.

"Well done," said Yanni. "Both of you. There isn't much we can do for you, except pass on the blessing that was given to us. You have a lot to find out, but trust each other and do what seems right, and all will be well for the island."

The girl was about to answer when she stiffened.

"Someone's watching us," she whispered.

The old couple glanced at each other. Yanni nodded.

"Yes," said Euphanie quietly.

"Is *she* here?" whispered the child.

"Not quite," said Euphanie. "Most of us here know the story. Many still believe it. Perhaps we are enough, gathered together like this, to bring an echo of her faintly back."

"Us and the owls," said Yanni. "We believe. They know."

The girl nodded and asked the question that had been on her lips, speaking without any hint of a stammer.

"Shall I be able to see in the dark?"

"Perhaps, provided you believe," said Euphanie.

# The Fifth Element

IN THE SLOW DUSK TYPICAL of the planet David carried the body back towards the camp. He was thinking not about its death, but about its name. Cat. Except for being roughly the right size it was nothing like a cat—a plump body covered with coarse gingery hair too sparse to conceal the folds and dewlaps of indigo flesh which sagged in a variety of curves according to the attitude the creature chose to lounge in. It was a not-quite-biped, with long forelimbs, three-fingered, and short hind limbs. It had no visible neck, but a hackle of black fur ran from its shoulders over the almost perfect sphere of its skull, stopping abruptly at the line which would have joined the centres of its round yellow eyes, whose double lids closed inwards from the sides. Its mouth was round too. It had no nose and no sense of smell, which made it one of the rare exceptions to the galactic norm of five senses for all higher creatures. (Not all had the same five, of course—the crew of David's ship disposed of nine, between them.) But then Cat was hardly a crew member, only a pet or mascot, really. David had never heard of a ship that didn't carry a Cat—that was odd, because he had never heard either of a Cat doing anything useful for a crew, and ships didn't normally lug waste weight round the galaxy, even the odd four kilos of Cat's body. It wasn't a normal kind of superstition either, half-mocked and half-revered. You didn't blame the Cat for a luckless voyage. You just took it along with you, and barely noticed it. By the time he reached the camp David was beginning to think that he should have noticed these oddities before. After all, it was his function to notice and remember facts and then to fit them into patterns.

He found a Bandicoot by the fire, curled asleep like an ammonoid fossil, but twitching violently with its dreams. Hippo was by the ship, rubbing her back against a support strut, like a cow scratching at a post.

"Hey, careful!" said David. "That strut's designed for most shocks, but not for that."

"Ooh, isn't it?" said Hippo, vaguely. "Sorry. I forgot. I'm itchy."

She trundled towards the fire and stood gazing pathetically at David with her large-fringed eyes, pinker than ever in the light of the flames. Hippo was better named than Cat. Coming from a large planet which was mostly glutinous swamp her species had evolved to a shape something like a terrestrial hippopotamus, only larger. Her head was different, with its big braincase and short prehensile trunk, but her eyes lay on its upper surface so that she tended to lower her head, as if shy, when talking to one. She was a lot of weight to ferry around, but less than her equivalent in tractors and carrying-machines; and she could seal off her huge lungs and work in vacuum conditions, or in noxious gases, for several hours at a time. Hippos came in a wide variety of colours. This one was pale yellow.

"Do you think I'm pregnant, Man?" she said. "That would be most inconvenient."

The lowered head made her look as though she should have been blushing as she spoke. David snorted with suppressed laughter.

"I don't think it's likely, darling," he said. "I know you go in for delayed implantation, but it must be a couple of years since you last went to a dance, isn't it?"

"But it would be inconvenient, all the same?"

"Understatement of the century."

Hippos were the kindest, gentlest, most lovable creatures David knew. This made their lifecycle seem even more horrifying than it was. At certain seasons on their native planet they would meet for a "dance", a massive sexual thresh-about in the sludge, with all the males impregnating all the females, if possible. Then nothing happened till the wind was right and the weather was right, when the females would go through their incredibly brief pregnancy, which would end with their backs erupting into a series of vents and releasing a cloud of seedlike objects, each consisting of a hard little nut at the core which contained the foetus and a fluffy ball of sticky filaments surrounding it, the whole thing light enough to float on the wind like thistledown. These "seeds" seemed to have some instinct that drew them towards living flesh; those that failed to find any perished, but those that landed on a warm-blooded animal stuck there and burrowed in, completing their foetal development inside the host, supplying themselves with all their physical and chemical needs from the host's organs. The host did not survive the process. The variety of possible hosts accounted for the different colours of Hippos.

David thought it extremely unlikely that this one was pregnant. For some reason he couldn't at the moment recall the maximum known period between fertilization and birth, but it couldn't possibly be two years. Surely not. But just supposing . . . the idea of surveying a planet in which Hippo spores might still be drifting on the wind made him shudder. And Hippo herself wouldn't be much use till her back had healed. He decided to change the subject.

"I'm afraid Cat's dead," he said.

"Oh dear, oh dear," said Hippo. "Where did you find him?"

"Out among the rocks over there. He must have been scrambling about and fallen, or something."

"Are you sure he's dead? Couldn't Doc do anything?"

"I doubt it. He feels very dead to me."

"Do go and fetch Doc, Man. Please"

"All right."

Doc was in a bad mood. As David lifted his bucket off its gimbals he put a hooter out of the water and said, "I thought you told me this wasn't an earthquake planet."

"Nor it is."

"Whole ship's been jumping around like a . . . Hi! Careful! You're going to spill me, you dry slob."

David ignored him, but carried the bucket rapidly through the shuddering ship till he reached the entry port.

"Hippo" he yelled. "Stop that! You'll have the ship over!"

Apologetically she moved away from the strut.

"Oh, I *am* sorry, Man," she lowed. "The Bandy should have told me."

"Didn't notice," squeaked the Bandicoot, awake now. "Why should I?"

"Where are the others, Bandy?" called David.

"Coming, coming," shrilled the Bandicoot.

Bandicoots were a four-sexed species, deriving from a planet so harsh that it took many square miles to support a single specimen. They had evolved great telepathic powers in order to achieve occasional meetings of all four sexes, and this made them an ideal communications network on the many planets where mechanical systems were swamped by local radio stars. David had no idea why they were called Bandicoots—they looked more like armadillos on stilts—and even after years of companionship he couldn't tell one from another. They could, of course, because the network only functioned at full strength when all four sexes took part. Their normal voices were far above David's hearing-range; the twittering he could just hear was for them the deepest of basses.

"Here's your patient, Doc," he said, settling the bucket by Cat's body.

Doc extended a pseudopod, shimmering orange with the firelight and green with its own luminescence, and made it flow up Cat's spine. His hooter emerged from the water.

"Blunt instrument," he said.

"Sure it wasn't a fall?" said David.

"Course I am, you idiot. It takes more than a fall to kill a Cat. You have to know exactly how and where to hit. Somebody did."

"Somebody?" said Hippo. "I thought there wasn't anybody on this planet. Skunk said so."

"How long ago, Doc?" said David. "Sure he's dead?"

"I'm still looking. H'm."

David had never much cared for Doc's bedside manner, but had always trusted him totally, as all the crew had to trust each other. Now he wondered how, that time he was infested with green-fever larvae out round Delta Orion, he could have lain so calmly and let Doc extend his filaments all through his body, locating and destroying the little wrigglers and modifying David's autoimmune system to produce antibodies against the bacteria they had carried. Doc was a sea anemone. The pseudopod he was using to explore Cat's body was a specialized section of his digestive organs, and the filament tips were capable of recognizing at a touch the identity of all the microscopic particles which he needed for the endless process of renewing every cell in his body once a week. Almost all Doc's life was taken up with the process of self-renewal, but he said it was worth the trouble because it made him immortal. It also made him a good doctor, when he could spare the time.

"Tsk, tsk," he said. "Yes, dead as nails, whatever they are. About twenty minutes ago."

"That's not long," said Hippo. "Can't you patch him up?"

"I'd have a go if it was you, darling," said Doc. "It's not worth the effort for a Cat."

"But you spent so much time looking after it," said Hippo, pleadingly.

"It was a lousy hypochondriac." said Doc. "I've got better things to do."

"Coming, coming," shrilled the Bandicoot.

"Hippo, get away from that strut," said David. "Find a tree or something."

"Trees on this planet are so feeble," said Hippo. "I've used up all that lot."

Through the remains of dusk David could see that the grove of primitive palms by which they had set up camp had considerably altered in outline. He remembered hearing a certain amount of splintering and crashing as he was walking back to camp.

"You'd better get Doc to have a look at you," he said. "Doc, poor Hippo's got an itchy back."

"Never get through that ugly thick hide," mumbled Doc "Got better things to do."

"I know it's nonsense, but I can't help thinking I'm pregnant," said Hippo.

"Get yourself an obstet . . . an obstet . . ." said Doc as he withdrew all but the limb of his pseudopod beneath the surface.

"Doc!" said David. "You aren't eating Cat!"

"Oh, no!" said Hippo, with all the revulsion, normally suppressed in her case, of herbivores for meat eaters.

"Doc!" shouted David.

The hooter came an inch out of the water.

"Lot of good stuff in there," said Doc, slurring the syllables until he was barely comprehensible. "No point wasting it. All these months, living on chemical soup."

"What about the Hippocratic oath!" said David.

"Coming, coming!" shrieked the Bandicoot, rising and jigging like a sandhopper on its spindly legs. Its cry was answered by another from the sky, and a moment later, with the usual blur and buzz of wings, Bird settled at the edge of the ring of darkness. The second Bandicoot dropped from her back and jigged across to join the first.

"Bandy said to skim home," said Bird in the metallic voice produced by moving one wing-case to make a flow of air and then modifying the flow with the sensitive leading edge of the wing itself.

"What's up, Man?" she added. "The Bandy told you about the wreck?"

"No. And I didn't say anything about bringing you home. The last my Bandy told me was about a seam of Sperrylite you thought you'd spotted. What kind of wreck? How old?"

Bird raised a wing-case and let it fall back, producing a sharp explosion like a mining blast. This was her form of swearing.

"I'll chop him up and feed him to my husband," she rasped.

She had met her "husband" in the larval stage, when they were both about three inches long, and after a brief, blind courtship had incorporated him in her body, where he now lay, like an extra gland, somewhere near the back of her four-foot thorax. Doc had once paid him a visit, out of curiosity, and said that there was still an intelligence there, of a sort, but that it spent all its time dreaming. He guessed that the dreams were nonrepresentational, but had never been able to interest Skunk or the Bandicoots in finding out. Bird was not merely a flying scout. She had evolved from a migratory species whose guidance system depended on their ability to sense the magnetic field of their planet with great accuracy; so now she was able, skimming on her gauzy wings above the surface of a strange planet, to map the irregularities where different metallic ores showed up. And in deep space she was like an old sailor with a weather eye, able to sense long before it registered on the instruments the coming of one of the particle-storms that could rush like a cyclone out of the apparently blank spaces between the stars.

"Yup, space wreck," she said. "More than a month old, less than a year. Real mess. Didn't go in, but my Bandy said he couldn't feel anybody thinking down there. I was just going to skim in close when he told me to hurry home. I was coming, anyway, but what made him do that?"

"Nothing, except Cat's dead."

"Somebody killed him," said Hippo.

"With a blunt instrument," said David.

Bird made a contemptuous rustle with her wing-cases, and before the sound had ended Mole came snouting out of the earth beyond the fire, shaking soil from his pelt like a dog shaking off water. As the flurry of pellets pattered down, the third Bandicoot scrambled out of the capsule which Mole trailed behind him on his subterranean journeys and skittered off to join the other two. Now all three were hopping like hailstones on paving, and shrilling at each other in and out of the limits of David's hearing range.

"What's up?" growled Mole.

"Cat's dead and I'm pregnant," said Hippo.

"I don't know why I bother," said Mole. "Soon as this trip's over I'm paying off and going home."

He would have trouble finding it, thought David. Home for Mole was somewhere in the Ophiucus area, a planet—or rather an ex-planet—which had become detached from its sun and all of whose life-forms had evolved in a belt between the surface permafrost and the central fires.

"Home?" said Bird. "Yup. Good thinking. Count me in on payday."

She clicked and tocked in a thoughtful way. Doc put his hooter up, sighed "Ho-o-o-ome," and plopped back under.

Home. Why not? Earth. Clothed, soft-skinned bipeds. David was a rich man, in theory, by now. He could afford to retire, buy four or five young wives and a mother-in-law, and a nice little island . . .

The Whizzers cut the reverie short by slithering into the camp, bringing the last of the Bandicoots. At once all thought and talk were impossible in the frenzy of jigging and shrilling, until Bird turned on the four of them and drove them, with a series of fierce explosions, round to the far side of the ship. Meanwhile Skunk crawled down from the Whizzer he had been riding. The Whizzers were legless reptiles from a planet of crushing gravity. They were about seven feet long and three feet wide, but less than a foot high, and on planets less massive than their own they could carry reasonable weights over almost any surface at speeds of up to sixty miles an hour. They flowed. David seldom got the chance to ride one, because his function was to stay at base and coordinate information with his own stored knowledge; but sometimes, when he needed to see something with his own eyes, a Whizzer had taken him and he had found the ride as much fun as surf boarding. Despite being hermaphrodites, Whizzers paired for life. They were deeply religious.

Skunk was also a hermaphrodite and legless, but otherwise nothing like a Whizzer—slow, sightless, a nude blob, corrugated with scent glands. He could synthesize and aim a jet of any odour he wished. He could stun even Hippo with a stink, provided her nostril was unsealed. On the anniversary of David's first joining the crew Skunk had presented him with a smell which was all the pleasures of his life, remembered and forgotten, linked into ten minutes of ecstasy. Skunk knew what odours to produce because he was a telepath, not in the style of the Bandicoots, but able to sense the minutest variations of emotion: thus he could attract or repel, numb or excite, at will. David had seen him organize the slaves of a fully functioning mine in Altair to load the ship with jade while their trance-held guards watched impotent. That had been a rich trip, if risky. Pity they'd had to trade the loot for fuel at a way station . . . Skunk had almost total power except over creatures such as Cats, which had no sense of smell. He could be any colour he chose. He could feel danger long before David could analyse it. Surface-scouting on a new planet was always done by a team of two Whizzers, one Bandicoot, and Skunk.

"The Bandicoot said we were to return," hissed one of the Whizzers. "What new providence has the Lord effected?"

"I don't know," said David. "I think that the Bandicoots just wanted to get together."

"Listen to them," said Mole.

"Disgusting," said the Whizzers.

"A very untidy relationship," said Bird, smugly.

"Dear little things," said Hippo.

"Hippo, get away from that strut," said David.

"Sorry," said Hippo. "You know, I really am pregnant."

"You and who else?" said Bird. "You aren't the only female in these parts, remember. There's me, too, and several halves and quarters."

"But it's important," said Hippo.

"It's hysterical," snapped Bird. "Get Doc to check. He'll tell you."

"Doc's drunk," said David. "He's found some substance in Cat's body . . . But if Hippo does give birth it means she'll produce a cloud of seeds which float about until they stick to a living body—then they burrow in and eat it out from the inside."

"Charming," said Bird. "What happens if they land on another Hippo?"

"Why do you think they've evolved that hide, and the ability to seal off?" said David.

"Well, we'll just have to copy her," said Bird. "Get inside the ship, seal off, and wait till the happy event is over."

"But you can't do that," said Hippo. "What about my babies? What will they eat?"

"Oh, they'll find something," said Bird.

"But was it not revealed to Brother/Sister Skunk that the Lord has not yet seen fit to bring forth warm-blooded creatures upon this planet?" said one Whizzer.

"Infinite is His mercy. Strange are His ways," said the other.

David started trying to work out whether Hippo could bust her way into the ship. His analysis wouldn't cohere. He didn't know how much extra strength to allow for the desperation of maternal feelings, and all the other constants seemed to be slithering around. Then, in the middle of this mess, a wholly irrelevant point struck him. He ought to have seen it before.

"That means one of us killed Cat," he said.

There was a sudden silence, apart from the climax of shrilling beyond the ship. Strange are His ways, thought David.

"Yes. Man," said Skunk in his laboriously produced groan. "Something. Odd . . . Cat. Dead . . . Must. Know. How . . . Why?"

"Sorry, I can't help," said David. "I don't know."

"Come off it," snapped Bird. "You've got to know. That's what you're there for, to classify and analyse information. That's why we bother to cart you around with us—it's your function."

"I'm afraid I'm not functioning very well today," said David.

"Feeling all right?" hooted Doc. "Like me to have a squint inside you?"

"Not on your life," said David. "I'm fine. Only . . ."

"Only you're not kissing well going to bother," said Bird.

"Sister Bird," hissed the Whizzers. "You must modify your language or we desert."

There was a moment of shock. Nobody ever deserted. Nobody ever joked about it. By the same token Bird always remembered not to swear in front of the Whizzers.

"Yet the Lord has revealed to Brother/Sister Skunk that the duty has fallen on us to discover how and why Brother Cat was called to his Maker," said one Whizzer.

"Blessed is His name," said the other.

"*All* right," said Mole, "let's go along with that. We can all analyse a bit, I suppose. We don't have Men around at home, do we? Doc, sober up and pay attention. Bird, go and see if the Bandies have finished whatever it is they do . . ."

David withdrew into himself. He was not Man, he was David. He felt enormous reluctance to take part in analytic processes. It didn't matter who had killed Cat, or why, and the others were only discussing it because Skunk said it was important—they were accepting Skunk's dictum out of habit, because they were used to the idea of Skunk being right about that sort of thing, just as they were used to the idea of Bird being right about the threat of a particle-storm. Those were part of their functions but it didn't mean that Skunk was in command—no one was, or they all were. They collected information through their nine senses, relayed it if necessary through the Bandicoots, and David collated it with what he knew and interpreted the resulting probabilities. Then, always till now, it had become clear what they should do next, and there had been no point on taking a vote, or even discussing the issue. They were a crew, a unit like a beehive or a termite nest. They had lost their previous Hippo because they'd landed on a quaking planet and the only way to take off from its jellylike surface was for that Hippo (a young one, male, mauve) to hold the ship upright from the outside while they blasted clear. At the time it had seemed sad, but not strange, to leave poor Hippo roasted there, and Hippo seemed to think so too. The Whizzers had sung a hymn as they'd blasted off, he remembered. But now . . .

Now he sat in the ring of creatures round the campfire and felt no oneness with them. They were aliens. They squeaked and boomed and lowed and rasped in words he could scarcely understand, though they were all speaking standard English. The fire reflected itself from the facets of Bird's eyes: her mandibles clashed like punctuation marks in the flapping talk from her wing-cases. Doc had withdrawn his pseudopod from Cat's drained body and the surface of his water was frothy with the by-products of his feast. The Bandicoots had joined the circle and were engrossed in the talk, all four heads perking this way and that as if joined by a crank-rod. The Whizzers lay half folded together, like a pair of clasped hands. Mole had absentmindedly dug himself down and was listening with his elbows at ground level and his snout resting on his little pink palms with their iron-coloured claws Skunk, too, had forgotten himself enough to be producing vague whiffs and stinks, as if trying to supplement the difficult business of speech with the communication system he used among his own kind.

I belong on Earth, thought David. What am I doing here? Being part of a crew, that's what. But what is the crew doing here? Prospecting, with a bit of piracy when the chance offers, that's what. But why? Why any longer? He was rich—they all were, enormously rich in the currency of their home planets. Or were they? All those claims. Were they valid? Had anyone exploited them? That jade, hijacked in Altair—a share of that would have been enough to buy David twenty wives and islands for all of them, but without argument they had traded it for less than a thousandth of its value in fuel—to what end? More exploration, more claims . . .

David knew all this quite well. It was part of his memory—of all their memories—and there had seemed to be quite good reasons for it at the time. None of them had been the real reason, the need to stay together as a crew . . . And now the knowledge and the memory were strange, as strange as the ring of aliens who had fallen silent and were staring at him—those that had eyes to stare with.

"Man," groaned Skunk. "Why. You. Kill. Cat?"

David barely understood the blurred syllables.

"Me?" he said. "Oh, rubbish. And my name's David."

"Come off it," clattered Bird. "It's got to be you. Doc was in his bucket, with no transport. Hippo was with the base-camp Bandy."

"The base-camp Bandy was asleep," said David. "Hippo could have done it."

"Do you really think so?" said Hippo.

"No. Go on, Bird."

"The rest of us were scouting, none alone. You were alone. You left the camp. Why?"

"I wanted to go over to the rocks. I can't remember why."

"Not functioning again?"

"I suppose so."

"Two possibilities suggest themselves. Either you are suffering brain damage, which would account for your failure to function, and your killing Cat, and your not remembering that you had done so or why you went to the rocks. Or you are functioning, killed Cat for your own reasons and are concealing this by pretending not to function."

"That's easy to check," said David. "Ask the Bandies. Am I functioning, Bandies?"

The eight eyes swivelled towards him on short stalks.

"Yesyesyesyes," shrilled the Bandicoots. "Man's functioning fine."

It was true. The hesitation, the slither, the blur of thought of the last two hours had been sucked away like mist sucked off autumn meadows by the sun, leaving the normal clarity of instant connections, of each detail of knowledge and experience available at the merest whisper of a wish. Except that in this shadowless illumination David could see for the first time that the state was not normal. It was what he was used to, yes; but for a member of the genus homo sapiens it was abnormal. The sapience had been distorted into grotesque growth, like the udder of a dairy cow.

"OK, I'm functioning now," he said. "But was I functioning when you got back to camp, Bandies?"

"Don't remember," they said. "Busybusybusy."

"Are we sure it matters?" said Hippo. "We've only lost a Cat, and look, we've got another one,"

David saw their heads turn, but himself, caught in the rapture of returned illumination, barely glanced at the newcomer crouching at the fringe of the circle of firelight. A large Cat, almost twice the size of the old one, sidled towards Doc's bucket, trailing one hind leg. It had a fresh wound in its shoulder. As Doc's glimmering pseudopod rose and attached itself to the wound, David placed these new facts in their exact locations on the harsh-lit landscape of his knowledge.

"Yes, it matters," he said. "Skunk was right. It matters immensely to all of us. Look at me. Did I kill Cat?"

He willed their attentions away from the wounded Cat and onto him.

"All right," he said. "You be the jury. You decide, You aren't my peers, any of you, because we're all so different, but we've got one thing in common which is more important than any difference. Now, listen. Think. There isn't much time. What's happened since sunset? Up to then we were all functioning normally. The survey parties were out. The reports were coming in, everything as usual. Then, just as it began to get dark, Bird found a wreck, and her Bandy didn't report it. Instead all three Bandies told their parties to come home. About the same time I got an urge to visit the rocks, where I found Cat's body. 1 got back and found Hippo scratching herself on a support strut and saying that she was pregnant. If that was true, it meant that she had delayed implantation for an incredible length of time. Next, Doc started eating Cat, instead of trying to restore him to life; he also complained about his hypochondria. Hippo was shocked, though she normally manages not to worry about the carnivores in the crew. As soon as Mole got back he started saying he wanted to go home, and Bird and Doc said the same, and the Bandicoots went into their mating behaviour, which they've never done before when we've been landed—though it's only natural that they should—the presence of a four is immensely stimulating to Bandies—and Bird swore in front of the Whizzers and the Whizzers complained, and I realized I'd stopped functioning . . . How are you feeling, Hippo?"

"How kind of you to ask," said Hippo, incapable of irony. "Yes, I'm afraid I may have been a wee bit careless and let myself get . . .

you know what. I think I'll probably pop later tonight, but if you all get aboard and close the ports and I go downwind you'll be quite safe. My poor darlings will just have to take their chance."

"Remember what she was saying twenty minutes ago?" said David.

"The Lord has changed her heart," said a Whizzer.

"Infinite is His mercy," said the other one.

"Do you still want to go home, Bird?" said David.

"Come off it. I notice you don't ask old Mole. Just because I'm female you pick on me for a moment of nostalgia, as if I was a brainless ninny all the time."

"But you're back to normal now? You too, Mole? And the Bandies? And me. But it isn't normal. We're all behaving in ways which are unnatural for our species. We're suppressing some parts of our behaviour and exaggerating other parts. It isn't normal for me to act like a fault-free computer. My brain has computer like abilities, but in order to function as a crew member I've had to adapt them. It isn't normal for Bandies not to mate whenever four of them meet, but they've suppressed that side of their behaviour. It's the same with all of us. Now think of the order of events: Cat dies; we stop being a crew and become individuals; a new Cat turns up and we start being something like a crew again; only this new Cat is badly wounded and not paying proper attention, which is why we have still got a little time left."

David glanced towards the bucket. The water level, which had at first perceptibly sunk was steady now. As soon as it started to rise it would mean that Doc was beginning to withdraw his substance from the Cat's body.

"Listen," he said. "Do you remember that load of jade we hijacked round Altair? We could all have retired on that, but we didn't. Instead we got rid of it at the first opportunity, for a ludicrous price. Why? Because it would have broken us up as a crew, and we've got to stay as a crew, not for our own sake but for Cat's. The Cat is a parasitic species. I don't know anything about natural Cat behaviour, which is interesting, considering that I've got all your details stored away, but my bet is that on their own planet Cats are parasitic on lower animals. When the first explorers reached their planet they simply adapted them into the system, and now the function of a space crew is to provide a safe environment for a Cat."

"It wasn't safe for our Cat," said Mole.

"It was almost safe. Between us we could control any normal dangers, except one. You missed a point in your analysis, you know. Doc said that if you're going to kill a Cat you have to know exactly where to hit. The only crew members who might have known were Doc and myself. Doc couldn't have got to the rocks, and I've already told you I don't know much about Cats, because our Cat never allowed me to. But there's one other creature who would have known, one creature whom neither Skunk nor the Bandies would have detected when they were feeling for traces of higher life on this planet. That's another Cat which survived the space wreck. A Cat large enough to ambush and kill our Cat despite a broken leg. Our Cat must have fought and wounded it, in the shoulder: our Cat must also somehow have mentally sent for me as the fight began, which was why I went out to the rocks, but I was too late."

David glanced at the bucket again. The water level had risen halfway to its normal level and the strange Cat was stirring.

"We've got to be quick," he said. "There's no time left. In a moment this new Cat will take us over. But we don't have to give in. Cats don't have total control. This one had to hang around and wait for the Bandies to finish their mating pattern, because that was an urge too powerful to be interrupted once it had begun. I don't think Cats are very intelligent—they don't have to be, because we do their thinking for them. But now we are aware what they do to us, I believe that we've got the will power and intelligence to resist the control, long enough to get clear. We can go home, find out if any of our claims are valid, and if they are we can retire. Surely we can cooperate that long, without being forced to by a Cat? You've got to make up your minds. Now, at once. That is part of the analysis. What's your verdict?"

The new Cat quivered, shook itself, and stood up by the bucket. Fresh scar tissue showed on its shoulder—so Doc had done a rushed job. The Cat took a pace towards the fire. If only it had a sense of smell, Skunk could have controlled it, But it hadn't. That too was part of the analysis.

"Quick. What's your verdict?" hissed David.

He felt the pressure of their attentions focused on him.

"Guilty," groaned Skunk. "Man. Guilty. Of. Mutiny."

David was only for an instant conscious of the blast of odour that laid him out.

He woke some time after midnight. The embers were dim, but gave just enough light for him to see that the ship's port was closed. Hippo was crashing around in the remains of the ruined grove. David rose, intending to go and say good-bye, but his legs walked him away from her—just as, a few hours back, they had walked him for no good reason towards the rocks. He was ceasing to function, but his normal intelligence was sound enough to tell him that he could never rejoin the crew, any crew, because his knowledge of the behaviour of Cats would henceforth be part of his memory and thus part of his function. He would not be able to perform his tasks without being aware of why he was doing so.

As the harsh clarity of thought faded into softer textures, full of vaguenesses and shadows, David became conscious of the planet around him, of the sweetness of its air, of the rustle of primitive leathery leaves, of the ticking insect life that might one day evolve towards a creature like Bird. He had known all these things, of course, soon after the ship had landed, but known them merely as facts—the chemical composition of the air, the level of evolution of plant and insect—and not as sensations, accepted and relished through channels other than those of the intellect.

Behind him the sound of splintering timber ceased. From vast lungs came a strange whinnying noise, dying into a long sigh. David realized he had been walking downwind from Hippo. His legs continued to do so. Breeze at, say, six kph—at any rate a little faster than he had been walking. He had about a kilometer start, so the seed cloud should reach him in . . . His mind refused to tackle even that simple sum, because it kept slithering off into irrelevancies, such as the sudden thought that Cats had five senses after all; and that they were more intelligent that he had guessed; and, to judge by their revenges, more catlike.